Venous Hum

VENOUS
HUM

SUZETTE MAYR

ARSENAL
PULP PRESS
Vancouver

ARSENAL PULP PRESS
103 – 1014 Homer Street
Vancouver, B.C.
Canada V6B 2W9
arsenalpulp.com

The publisher gratefully acknowledges the support of the Canada Council for the Arts and
the British Columbia Arts Council for its publishing program, and the Government of Canada
through the Book Publishing Industry Development Program for its publishing activities.

Design by Solo
Cover photography by Nicki Pardo / Getty Images

Printed and bound in Canada

This is a work of fiction. Any resemblance of characters to persons
either living or deceased is purely coincidental.

Efforts have been made to locate copyright holders of source material wherever possible.
The publisher welcomes hearing from any copyright holders of material used in this book
who have not been contacted.

Library and Archives Canada
Cataloguing in Publication

Mayr, Suzette
Venous hum / Suzette Mayr.

ISBN 1-55152-170-9

I. Title.

PS8576.A9V45 2004   C813'.54   C2004-902946-0

ACKNOWLEDGMENTS

I would like to thank Nicole Markotić, Rosemary Nixon, Blaine Kyllo, and Brian Lam for their editorial expertise and support.

A big thank you to the following people for letting me go to their high school reunions, both literally and figuratively, and for being so generous with their time: Peter Oliva, Alfi Forsch, Julien Mayr, Margo Fearn, Heather Johnston, and Bridget Saunders.

I am grateful to Rose-Marie and Ulrich Mayr for the histories, Hiromi Goto for *Chorus of Mushrooms* and cannibalism, and Lisa Brawn for the title and predator animal card.

For the extremely important miscellaneous, thank you to Cliff Lobe, Renée Lang, Friedrich Mayr, Wendy Beaver, Sally Chivers, Joanne Pohn, Keith Miller, Barb Scott, Julia Gaunce, Fred Wah, Jacqueline Larson, Jodey Castricano, Stefanja Dumanowski, Rebecca McEvoy-Halston, Candace Kootenay, Nancy Jo Cullen, Josette Leblanc, Emmelyne Callizaire, Lynn Sloane, Joss Whedon, and the griffin of Greifswald, Germany.

Thank you to the school teachers who were, fortunately, nothing like the teachers in this book: Christiane Abdel-Kader, Marguerite Dodds-Belanger, Jim Elliott, Mr Masson, Mlle Chamberlain, and Budge Burrows.

Thank you to the Markin-Flanagan Writer-in-Residence Program at the University of Calgary for giving me the time, space, and resources to complete the writing of this book.

I would like to thank Employment Insurance Canada and the Alberta College of Art and Design for funding this project in part.

Thank you to Blaine and Brian at Arsenal Pulp Press and my agent, Sally Harding, for taking the chance.

A final, special thank you to Tonya Darlene Anne Callaghan.

I am indebted to the following texts: *Trudeau and Our Times* by Stephen Clarkson and Christina McCall; "The Dead Are Trying to Reach Us" from *Big Ideas* by Lynda Barry; *Alberta: A New History* by Howard and Tamara Palmer; and *Mavericks: An Incorrigible History of Alberta* by Aritha van Herk. Recipes respectfully adapted from recipes by James Lee and Craig Claiborne.

Portions of this novel have appeared, in earlier form, in *Tessera* magazine.

For my parents, Rose-Marie and Ulrich

Dear Ann Landers:

*May I have the last word about high school
reunions? Our local school had a reunion
celebrating the school's hundredth anniversary,
and every graduate was invited. At the cocktail
party, I ran into a classmate who had made my life
a living hell during that time. I couldn't believe it,
but after twenty-five years, he apologized to me for
the agony he had put me through in high school.
People should attend their high school reunions.
They can give you a real lift. Mine certainly did.*

Signed, Chipper in New York

*"Florence Nightingale was a cannibal,
you know."*
– The Edible Woman, *Margaret Atwood*

In December 1967, Pierre Trudeau as Justice Minister of Canada presented the House of Commons with a divorce reform bill and amendments to the Criminal Code liberalizing restrictions on abortion and homosexuality. Borrowing from Martin O'Malley in *The Globe and Mail*, Trudeau said, "The state has no place in the bedrooms of the nation," and the beds of many nations promptly spun out of control.

In 1971, Pierre Elliott Trudeau, as Prime Minister of Canada, brought in an official Policy of Multiculturalism that proclaimed, Bonjour, You are invited, Hello, Vous êtes invités, to the thousands of non-European immigrants who had been flooding the country since the early 1960s. Those who never felt comfortable suddenly were *home*. At the time, Trudeau sported a long, flowing haircut.

Canada's hair has been disheveled ever since.

PROLOGUE

The dreams worry her. Her mother is a skilled dream interpreter.

Teeth. Teeth falling out means mortality. One death for each tooth. The closer the teeth to the front of the mouth, the younger the person who'll die.

Vomiting. Well, that's purging. Like finally telling your youngest sister, the one with the leather heart, you don't love her and that you haven't loved her for *years*.

Shit. Shit means money. If you dream you're having a bowel movement and you produce a stool that means you're making money or you're going to make money. Blood in the stool? No explanation needed.

Lai Fun's dreams contain no easy symbols like teeth or puke or shit. She dreams she's put in a load of laundry, the one that's been in the basket for three days. She dreams she's spoken to Eugene at work about the phrasing for a special general meeting announcement: "Staff are expected to attend a special general meeting this Thursday. Location: Room s317. Time: 4:30 PM *sharp*." She dreams she's unscrewed the p-trap under the kitchen sink with a wrench and cleaned out the gobs of hair, phoned in an order for flowers for her mother's birthday and asked the florist who sounds like Joni Mitchell to put it on her credit card, put on the white blouse hanging in her closet because it's the only one that doesn't need to be re-ironed. The dreams wake her with their banality. She contemplates the ceiling in the dark, then realizes she is only dreaming that she contemplates the ceiling in the dark.

Lai Fun dreams she's sent email at work. She dreams about the soy milk in her fridge: a carton of vanilla-flavoured *So Good* soy milk stands on the first shelf in her fridge next to the jar of ancient olives.

Really, what is the point of dreaming at all?

Perhaps her subconscious fear of being found out as a fake or a prude or at heart a boring person is welling to the surface. Perhaps she feels guilty for being such an imperfect, impatient mother. Except that she isn't a mother. It all makes sense in the dreams. Perfect, banal sense.

Lai Fun doesn't mean to be ungrateful – she could have recurring nightmares, she could have insomnia, she could have bigger problems like dreaming in a war-zone – it's just that the dreams confuse her now. Did she remind Jennifer to make that phone call to the fertility clinic or did she just dream it? Did she really borrow Edward the commissionaire's pencil? Most of the time she's sure. Most of the time.

It's not that the dreams frighten her. It's just that dreams about tea bags are so – *soggy*.

Then two months before her wedding she dreams about the stone griffins on the Centre Street bridge downtown – the muscles sculpted into their stone haunches, their lion's claws gripping the stone, the river simmering beneath them – griffins not like the regular monsters children hide under their beds or in their bedroom closets – the vampires, the werewolves, even the zombies. The griffins are much older, more complicated than these. Eagle and lion fused to make *what*?

Lai Fun's eyes roll in her sleep.

The griffins watched Lai Fun, a soft-boned blob in her mother's arms, the day her father first drove her home from the General Hospital. For almost forty years, they watched Lai Fun's school bus rides to elementary school, her mopey walks to high school, and later her drives home from work. The petrified gloss of their beaks, their feathers, the cold damp of their breaths. Turned into stone mid-scream.

I dreamed about the griffins on the Centre Street bridge, she tells her mother on the phone.

Griffins? Louve says. I don't know what *that* means. They're rebuilding that bridge and getting rid of the griffins. They were put up before there even *was* a city. The assholes in this city don't care about anything old. Months and months of dreams about lawn-mowing and grocery lists, and now you want me to interpret monsters? A monster is a monster is a monster. Your dream is warning you to watch out for monsters. When you get married, Godzilla's going to be a third cousin twice removed! Ha ha ha!

We could write a letter to City Council. Talk about maintaining the city's heritage. Respecting public art, says Lai Fun, violently brushing the cat.

She never cared that much about those griffins before they invaded her dream, but she does not like change. Change irritates her. Clumps of cat hair drift up her nose, waft into her hair. The cat purrs and stretches into a crescent.

I've got my own battles to deal with right now, says Louve. I can't go taking on that one.

Louve, phone tucked between her shoulder and her ear, sweeps her paint-brush across a piece of cardboard: "Make Love Not Implosions." She paints the first three words in a block letters, the last in cursive letters. She paints a tiny skull and crossbones at centre bottom.

But it's not bad to dream about griffins so close to the wedding, right? My dream wasn't about *any* monster, it was about *those* monsters on *that* bridge.

Probably all that Italian bread you ate. I don't know why you always have to fill up on the bread. The wedding will outdo Princess Diana's, honey. As long as it doesn't rain. That's bad luck. Rain on your wedding day. What rhymes with "Implosions"?

It's the first time Louve has used the word "wedding," and Lai Fun believes she has the best mother ever. Although the reference to Princess Diana's is not so good.

Louve tries to pick one of her own hairs out of the paint of the skull and crossbones. It streaks a tiny vein from "Love" into "Make." Maybe she should leave the hair in for effect.

Lai Fun starts writing a letter to City Council about the griffins, but then in the middle of her first paragraph, third sentence, right after the word "yes," she finds out her best friend from high school, Stefanja, is pregnant because Stefanja and her husband got pissed on ouzo one afternoon and lost control. Stefanja's news makes Lai Fun feel like someone's peed into a paper cup and given it her to hold. Stefanja doesn't even like ouzo. It's Lai Fun who's dying for a baby! Is there no order in the world?

I thought you'd be happy, says Stefanja. Lai Fun's letter to save the griffins flutters away in the face of cat hair and pregnant neighbours.

No woman at Stefanja's age gets pregnant by accident, says Louve, phone receiver in the crook of her neck. She's trying to save that marriage.

Louve's mouth is wide open as she glues on her false eyelashes. She is late for work. Late. Now is no time for talking on the phone to sterile, hysterical daughters.

But then Thomas Singh's sperm takes and Lai Fun becomes pregnant too and Lai Fun no longer feels betrayed, she feels like they are sisters again, she and Stefanja, and that their children will grow up as cousins.

Stefanja decides to skip the prenatal classes because Guatemalan peasants and Cro-Magnon women didn't take prenatal classes and they managed to give birth just fine. Jennifer has brought home all the books to Lai Fun; taking prenatal and parenting classes are a given, Jennifer insists. Stefanja's pregnancy makes Lai Fun pick at her cuticles. She tries not to be sarcastic when Stefanja can't get over her own blossoming nipples. Which Stefanja would know all about if she was taking a prenatal class.

It's like they grew in one morning! says Stefanja, her blouse hiked up around her neck. Literally! Are your nipples this big? I put on my bra in the morning, they're regular size, I take off my bra when I come home from work, and I've got a pair of diamond-hard, King Kong eyeballs staring at me in the mirror!

Like Stefanja is the only woman on the planet to go through premature pregnancy nipples or something. Lai Fun stares at her brown pinhead nipples and stupidly flat stomach. She stares and stares until she realizes a guy walking his poodle on the street is staring too.

Stare at poodle tits much? she shouts out the window and scoops the drapes closed.

Lai Fun will be pregnant at her wedding. Jennifer Singh thinks this is very funny. We're having a shotgun wedding, Jennifer tells their friends at the Lesbian Mothers' support group, on the links before she clocks her ball into the rough, Jennifer's black and white leather shoes glitter in the sun. Lai Fun sweeps her ball onto the green. The baby has made her into some kind of Tiger Woods, while Jennifer has become obsessed with mucous plugs and wedding cakes and polishing shoes. Jennifer toys with the idea of having an empty rifle beside them at the altar, maybe with a giant big bow on the safety – pink, it's bound to be a girl – and a chrysanthemum stuffed into the muzzle.

Lai Fun says, No.

Because Jennifer wanted a baby and Lai Fun wanted a baby but Lai Fun didn't want a baby out of wedlock. This made Jennifer's mouth bust out laughing and Lai Fun said, What's so funny?

Like them getting married to stop their child from being born a bastard was an unreasonable request.

We can have a baby if we get married, repeats Lai Fun.

Jennifer says, Okay. Will you marry me? then coughs to clear the laugh-mucous from her throat.

I will marry you, says Lai Fun. Yes. Good. We're going to have a baby! she says, and swings her arms around Jennifer.

Lai Fun doesn't mention that Jennifer once told her she might have to trade Lai Fun in for a newer model if Lai Fun didn't have a baby soon. Which made Lai Fun want to strangle Jennifer.

They crackle popcorn into their mouths for a minute or two and then Jennifer stands up from the couch.

Guess what? Jennifer whispers into Lai Fun's ear.

What? Lai Fun whispers back.

You're going to be a daddy!

Yeah well, I'm not wearing pink or *anything* made of velour.

You have to eat meat now.

No, says Lai Fun.

You have to.

Will not.

Fish?

No. My parents pumped me full of meat when I was a kid. I have enough meat in my system for four sets of quintuplets. My bottle was filled with beef blood, not milk. This baby is not going to be some kind of meat-eating, Rosemary's baby with horns and talons.

Who was talking about horns and talons? asks Jennifer.

You telling me to eat meat!

And while Jennifer catches up on her email and drafts up memos, Lai Fun gulps half a glass of cow's milk because Jennifer likes cow's milk in her morning coffee even though Lai Fun has asked her nicely, *so nicely*, to try soy milk just *once*. Lai Fun hasn't tried to drink cow's milk in years. Halfway through the glass she remembers that cow's milk is full of cow-pus.

We could pretend to make a baby right now! calls Lai Fun, scrubbing at her mouth with a dish-cloth.

Lai Fun asks Angélique, her sister the lawyer: Is it unreasonable to want to get married before we have a baby?

Angélique laughing and laughing and laughing at the other end of the phone because Lai Fun doesn't want the baby to be a bastard. Isn't that *cute*. Angélique mopping up the scattered bits of laughter, saying, That's sweet, like those sweet little pickles!

Angélique finishes off her laughing with, I'll have that file ready for you next week, code for: One of the partners just walked in and I haven't billed enough hours this month.

Lai Fun doesn't think Angélique's that funny. It's not so unreasonable not to want your child to be a bastard. Angélique is a lesbian. She thinks Angélique of all people should understand.

Not that Jennifer's parents would attend the wedding anyway. Jennifer's brother will, he thinks they think he's the king of the hour. It's his sperm they impregnated Lai Fun with after all, so they could both be blood related to the baby. They've been kissing his ass for almost eight months now because the sperm didn't take the first seven times.

The ceremony, the photos, the reception will be at Hotel Macdonald because Lai Fun has always wanted to throw a party at the Macdonald with its sandstone magnificence. For years she has looked at the gold-leaf, sculpted ceilings when she and Jennifer go there for their anniversary martinis; the chandeliers, the plush carpets covered in giant roses, the gold-rimmed mirrors, the dark, polished marble she can't resist caressing as she passes. One of the oldest, most beautiful buildings in the city. The château on the river. They will match the font on the place-cards with the font on the front of the building. They will both wear roses in nearly full bloom as corsages on their matching, raw silk skirt-suits. Lai Fun wanted them to match, and they do, almost, except Jennifer's suit is silver with red trim and Lai Fun's is red with silver trim. If they both wear skirts no dork can make dumb comments about who's the femme and who's the butch. Their champagne rose corsages will also match the roses on the carpets. The wedding will be perfect, and it's all Lai Fun's fault.

The night òf their wedding, at the reception in the Hotel Macdonald, Lai Fun can't drink because she's pregnant. Jennifer's still giggling at the shotgun nature of the ceremony. Lai Fun can't drink at her own wedding and she would like to crush the glass of sparkling water in her hand. She would love a glass of red wine, the light buzz that goes along with a cold beer, the smooth lurch in her throat from the juniper berries in a gin and tonic. A scotch. Her mouth *craves* a glass of *scotch*.

You can have one glass of something alcoholic, says Stefanja who has lumbered over like a beautiful beluga in her pink, see-through dress and blue pumps. Her dress is puffy and light and pink and New York. Her legs flex too many muscles and tendons. Her pie-sized nipples and sassy belly-button shout at Lai Fun through the fabric. Her belly is the moon.

You can have one glass of stout at your own wedding, for example, says Stefanja, sipping from one herself. Expectant mothers in Ireland drink lots of stout. Or a glass of red wine. Lots of iron in wine. Good for the baby.

What about ouzo?

What?

You can drink *one* drink, says Angélique. Angélique, Lai Fun's own *sister*, who is wearing a snow-drift white, cocktail-length, *vintage wedding dress* even though Lai Fun told Angélique

about her red suit, even though Lai Fun mentioned to Angélique that she, Lai Fun, Angélique's *baby* sister, was the one getting married.

No.

It's a party! It's *your* party! No wonder you had no friends
in high school.

Angélique! says Louve, a glass of white wine in one hand
and a scotch in the other. Leave your sister alone.

What! Wine's technically fruit juice.

Tonight her mother has a lovely glass of white wine in her
left hand, her nails, painted and reflecting the chandelier lights,
the lights shimmering off everybody's drinks. The scotch for
Fritz-Peter in Louve's other hand, the soft clink of the ice, that
earthy smell, like getting into bed in newly-washed pyjamas.
Lai Fun gets herself another glass of sparkling water from the
bar and shoves a Piña Colada with a paper cocktail umbrella
stuck into a slice of orange and a maraschino cherry at Jennifer,
who's finally finished her cigarette.

Here, says Lai Fun. But your Piña Colada has no scotch in
it.

I don't like scotch, says Jennifer, her corsage a bit crooked.
You like scotch.

Yes, says Lai Fun. But I'm pregnant. I can't drink. I've chosen to drink a virgin scotch. Your drink is pretty and would taste
even better with some scotch in it. I could absorb the scotch
through your kisses.

Jennifer sucks from the straw. Do virgin scotches have
scotch in them? she asks.

Yes, but it's pretend scotch.

Lai Fun puts her lips on the edge of her glass and inhales
pretend oak barrels and peat.

Look, says Jennifer, Maddie and Helen came.

They've been together forever, says Lai Fun. Having them
at our wedding is good luck. It's good luck, right, Mama?

Louve is tying a gold balloon to Fritz-Peter's lapel.

I want to be together forever just like them, says Jennifer. Just like your parents. That's what I want.

Lai Fun slips her arm around Jennifer's silver silk waist.

Lai Fun escorts Jennifer to her seat at the head table and, gallant and expert, pulls out a chair for her new wife. Then Lai Fun sits down and swirls the ice in her sparkling water with her finger. Jennifer gets up and heads to the bar for another drink and gets so busy talking to the bartender she misses the soup – Indonesian squash made with coconut milk and curry.

Jennifer makes it in time for the salad: blueberry vinaigrette on mixed organic greens and chilled asparagus with a sliced strawberry garnish. The guests clink their glasses with their cutlery and shout Kiss! Kiss! and Jennifer answers her cellphone. Lai Fun laughs until she sees Jennifer is actually talking into her phone. She has more pretend scotch.

Jennifer heads over to the bar for more drinks and stays so long she misses half the main course: marinated and roasted eggplant, peppers, asparagus, and tofu with garlic potatoes and daal on the side.

Lai Fun stomps up from her table and heads to the bar.

Jennifer! she says. Sit! Eat!

Lai Fun! says Jennifer. This is Headley Waterstone! Remember I mentioned him?

Mr Waterstone, says Lai Fun. Wonderful to meet you! Mr Waterstone, Jennifer. Your dinners are getting cold. Come eat! You can talk business later, yes?

Yes, says Mr Waterstone.

Mr Waterstone and I are just going to grab a quick smoke outside, says Jennifer.

So Lai Fun shuts up and stomps back to the table because Headley Waterstone is at her wedding and Jennifer must be peeing her skirt and would pee her skirt even more if she could get Headley Waterstone on the Board of Directors for

Gargoyle Communications. It would be a veritable coup. Just like the vegan wedding cake Lai Fun will eat alone.

Lai Fun wonders if everyone is enjoying their food as much as she is. She watches her mother tear into the eggplant with her fork and knife and teeth – her mother has such big, Kennedy teeth. Her father jams asparagus spears into his mouth with his long fingers. Angélique in her wedding cocktail frock sips her drink, pokes at the food with her fork, sips some more, lets the waiter clear away her full plate. Lai Fun sits alone at the head table and slices off a tiny piece of eggplant, takes a sip of her water. All the guests have finished their plates while she's been running around trying to lasso Jennifer back to the table. Lai Fun rests her hand on her stomach like pregnant women do in the movies, her stomach suddenly thick and hard in the last week. Breasts like bullets. She chews her eggplant and studies the gold and plaster vine leaves twining around the ballroom ceiling.

For dessert: zucchini carob cake made with soy milk, drizzled with a raspberry coulis.

Where's Jennifer? asks Louve. She leans down towards Lai Fun and Lai Fun can smell her mother's smell: *Souciant* perfume, chamomile talcum powder, lipstick, a brush of white wine. I need someone to go for a smoke with me. Honey, I don't want to criticize, this wedding has been a lot of fun –

There it is, Lai Fun's mother using the word "wedding" again!

– but why are the griffins off the Centre Street bridge part of the decorations? Did you buy them? Aren't they more appropriate for a garden setting? Are griffins some kind of gay symbol like the rainbow?

Lai Fun looks at the flaking, cracking griffins flanking the bar. Who invited *them*? She will find out later. Perhaps when she is in jail for murdering Jennifer on their wedding night. Gay symbols?

I think Jennifer's already smoking out back, says Lai Fun. I don't know. How would I know. I'm just her husband.

I'll find her, says Louve. Lovely event, Noodle.

Yes, says Lai Fun, smiling her special smile, the one she wears when she has to fire people, and she grabs Stefanja on her way to the bathroom for another pee.

You know, I wasn't going to tell you this, but weddings are only fun if they're not yours, calls Lai Fun from her stall.

That's what honeymoons are for, Stefanja says, and flushes. Thor and my wedding was like Christmas and Valentine's Day in one, but I sure was glad when it was over. We were *lucky*.

Well, Jennifer's going to have to a buy a truckful of Valentine's spackle to patch up this shit, says Lai Fun. She grabs at the cloud of toilet paper spinning from the holder. And we're not going on a honeymoon. Jennifer can't miss work.

Stefanja flushes a second time.

We're not even staying overnight in the hotel because Jennifer has work to do, says Lai Fun. The only reason I'm being nice to her is because she's my boss.

The *only* reason? says Stefanja.

That's *it*, says Lai Fun.

Let me get you a double pretend-scotch.

Lai Fun sees Jennifer talking to Maddie and Helen at their table and Jennifer laughs and her hair swept up in the back and falling down in the front all curly like that looks really good, so Lai Fun forgives her and blames her rage on the carbonation in the water she's been drinking all night.

Jennifer, she says. I'm going to go home. You can stay if you want.

Jennifer's hair perfect and falling into her eyes, her lips red and parted from the excitement of hanging out with Maddie and Helen, scoring Headley Waterstone for the Board of Directors, a glass of beer in her hand, and their very funny shotgun lesbian wedding. A gold balloon plucked from the wall and tied to the back of her jacket, bobbing around her head. She sweeps Lai Fun into her arms and kisses her – her breath has that bachelor, cigarette-and-beer taste.

Okay, Noodle. A great wedding if I say so myself, says Jennifer.

Lai Fun belches carbonated water.

Stefanja and Lai Fun wander through the underground parkade for twenty minutes hunting for Lai Fun's car. Lai Fun's high heels bite into her toes, rose corsage on her shoulder like a giant blossoming vagina, fetus squiggling inside her, Stefanja's squiggling too. Stefanja sweaty and peppy and fanning the wedding program in her face, babbling and chirping on about how motherhood has swept through her like the Christmas spirit, every day has been Christmas during her pregnancy – she even does a turn and the pink dress swirls up and Lai Fun can see Stefanja's matching pink maternity thong. Lai Fun wants to slap Stefanja silly, but that would be wrong. When they get to the house they sit on the bed and eat hot toast smeared with lots of margarine.

So Kim didn't come? asks Stefanja. She has slipped off her shoes and lies back into the pillows, a towel draped over her to prevent the margarine from dripping on her bubble of a dress.

RSVPed no, lies Lai Fun.

Hmph. I guess she doesn't know how important you are in the grand scheme of things.

Apparently not.

What about Lloyd Weaselhead?

You wanted me to invite him. I don't care about Lloyd Weaselhead. I was just kidding about Lloyd Weaselhead.

I think he would have appreciated it. Not having seen us since high school.

This was my wedding, not your high school reunion.

Jennifer Singh comes home at 4:03 AM and falls forward on the bed still in her silver suit and her matching high-heels.

25

Jennifer Singh has beautiful, thick hair, even when it's damp and disheveled from sweating and dancing and drinking with her buddies on her wedding night. The rose on her shoulder is missing half its petals, a burst balloon trails from her ass like toilet paper stuck to a shoe.

I guess I'll go home, says Stefanja, looking at Jennifer's heels aimed straight up at the ceiling.

Blink the light when you're inside.

Lai Fun watches Stefanja from her front step. Watches the porch light blink on off, on off.

Lai Fun pregnant with Freddy, Stefanja pregnant with Olivia. Lai Fun looks at Jennifer snoring her gluey snores with her shoes still on. Two months after Lai Fun dreamed the stone griffins on the Centre Street bridge and then they invited themselves to her wedding.

PART I

DEAR ANN LANDERS

CHAPTER 1

She pulls on her cotton underwear, pulls up her stockings, pulls at her skirt, pulls down her guilt, tucks up her bra, tucks in her shirt, tucks in her shame, walks out the door, her briefcase in hand, closes the door so quietly because he is sleeping, he is snoring and wearing a mere sheet tossed around him even though the room is minus 100 degrees Celsius and there was no time for a shower because she wasted too much time listening to him argue against the right to abortion and she will have to wash the smell of that wasted time off her (*his* mother wanted to abort *him* when she first got pregnant – what if she'd had easy access?), that and the smell of his sweat rushing off him and onto her in waterfall sheets, his saliva, the burn of his stubble even though she'd ordered him to shave before their lunch today and he said he would but of course he didn't. Who listens to her? He offered to shave in the hotel bathroom, but by then it was time for her to go back to work, this whole story so boring, so clichéd, so tired, so sordid, so obvious, so inevitable that writers can never leave it alone: she slept with him, then he slept with her, then she slept with her, then she slept with him, his red knees poking out from under the savaged sheets, the high colour in her cheeks, the suppleness in her joints, es-pecially around the pelvis, and then the fingers start waggling in judgment and the secrets strip like skin off a hip-bone, all arteries and veins exposed and bloody and babies and parents come pouring out in the ridiculous flood of gossip and flayed feelings. Who cares? Lai Fun stamps down the stairs. Why does anyone have to care?

All she needs is a little skin. She needs her skin fix and except for the times when he wants to *talk*, he gives it to her without any fuss, all she has to ask is, What're you doing at 2:45 this afternoon? and he says, Nothing, and she says, Good, I have half an hour, and her fix is set. It isn't human to go so long without a bit of skin. So he calls himself an artist when he hasn't produced any decent art, so she has to fight to keep her mouth shut when he blabbers on about what a caring and careful husband he is to his wife while he's in the middle of fucking *her*, she doesn't want real life in the room with them, she does not want conversation and caring to pollute what they do. She knows he watches himself when he fucks her, watches the muscles in his arms as he tosses her around on top of him and underneath him, slides her around like she is a wiener in a bun on a cart downtown. Watching the dollops of sweat drop from his forehead onto her chest.

But he is convenient and close by. He makes her cold skin tepid. She is ashamed of her need to be warm, but she is a fly on the windowsill in January. She has to survive. What is her pur-pose, really? Good wife, good mother, good employee? These are words they use in movies and magazines, but how do you verb the adjective "good"? At any other job she would expect a clear, precise list of her responsibilities. What about when she wishes her son – for whom she would throw herself in front of fourteen cars – would just leave her alone, leave her to her body just by itself, just for her? Why isn't she with him now?

That scrubbed smell of hotel because he says he's tired of

having to clean the sheets before his wife gets home. She pays on the way out, flashes her credit card and the room is paid, she's had her fix, she won't have to think about skin, about warmth, about marriage, child, until –

Lai Fun's sex with Stefanja's husband clutches at her heart with sludge fingers; Lai Fun *is* someone else's paper-cup of pee. When she leaves him and his smell still on her skin and she can taste his tongue in her mouth, when she can't stand it any more and they have time-annihilating, lacerating arguments about annual versus semi-annual car tune-ups, privatized health care (she grabs his blabbering mouth and slams him down on the bed), she chews her fingernails, chews like she hasn't chewed since she was sixteen and in love with the most popular girl in high school. Stefanja doesn't love him, they're only together for their daughter Olivia, she's told Lai Fun this over and over again, maybe she actually said I'll love him for Olivia, but Lai Fun doesn't remember the exact details, something about staying together because of the baby, they're only together for the baby; Lai Fun also recalls that Jennifer Singh hasn't noticed a thing about Lai Fun since the last chinook wind four months ago when Jennifer kissed Lai Fun's neck and then fell asleep.

I dreamed of a tray of pins, says Lai Fun. What does that mean?

Would it be too late to call and ask her mother?

Goodnight, says Jennifer. Jennifer kisses Lai Fun just above her left collar-bone, strokes her stomach once, and falls asleep.

Lai Fun is doing no one major harm, she is just looking out for her own sexual well-being. She only caves in once a week. Okay, this week twice. Twice a week was what she and Jennifer once managed. Twice a year the most Jennifer can manage now. So Lai Fun works three mornings and the rest of the time gives her life to Freddy. Lai Fun is pregnant again from another batch of sperm from Jennifer's brother – three weeks pregnant, so says the blue wand, so says her constant belching. Lai Fun feels sweaty and cold at the same time because as a rule she doesn't like sleeping with men. They are all right as sperm donors emptying themselves into carefully sterilized cups. They are all right as brothers-in-law, salesmen, actors, dentists, and postmen, but not for sex. Stefanja's Thor is not for sex.

She folds herself down on to the kitchen floor next to Baby Freddy. She rubs her hands over her face, runs her fingers over the pouches under her eyes, the tired, drooping skin around her mouth. She must be a good wife and mother and friend and kill this relationship. Take its throat in her hands and –

The phone rings. She looks up at the call display on the counter, her fingers on her own throat because it's Stefanja calling her about Thor. Baby Freddy squawks. Lai Fun reaches over and picks up the phone.

Lai Fun! says Stefanja.

Yes?

Lai Fun will answer Stefanja's questions sincerely and authentically. She will put her head in her hands as Stefanja rains down the telephone blows.

Kim's dead! says Stefanja.

Lai Fun looks at Freddy, who nods, then bangs a partially open bag of dry cat food on the floor.

What? Kim who?

Kim Shisamoto. You remember. You invited her to your wedding.

Huh?

Grade Twelve Physics. The G-Force incident. We hung out with her. *That* Kim. Lai Fun! How could you forget? She died of cancer. Come over.

Later. Lai Fun will have to confess her crimes to Stefanja later.

Lai Fun runs over with Freddy under one arm, his fists and face covered in cat food crumbs, the bag of cat food under her other arm, even though she is so tired from work and her lunch date with Thor and her adulterous regret she wants to slash her own jugular. Because Stefanja is her best friend since high school. Because Stefanja thinks Kim was too. Lai Fun can't say no even though she is dying to say no, she would give up her first born, Freddy (named after a famous homosexual Prussian king, though her mother refuses to acknowledge this), just to say no, just to have a nap in her own bed for ten minutes, just ten minutes. She throws up into Stefanja's toilet carefully, thoughtfully, quickly. Which is what the prenatal classes tell her happens to over-tired, hungry pregnant women. What Lai Fun could tell you about hunger!

Lai Fun rinses out her mouth with water and mouthwash, then cleans cat food out of her son's mouth with her fingers and a wet cloth, brushes cat food out of her son's hair, wipes the crumbs off his face with her hands, then with the cloth. She reads the ingredients list on the side of the cat food bag: Chicken By-Product Meal, Dried Egg Product, DL-Methionine, Chorine Chloride, Inositol, Potassium Iodide, Cobalt Carbonate. She wonders if she should make Freddy chew some charcoal.

Why? asks Stefanja, her eyes dribbling tears, deep frown wrinkles around her mouth.

Her father always made Lai Fun chew charcoal when her stomach hurt, like the time when she ate half a jar of tropical fish food.

Why not? asks Lai Fun, irritated that Kim had to choose *now* to die. Stefanja, you're crying!

Lai Fun plucks a paper towel from Stefanja's counter and hands it to her to wipe away the tears.

She's heard of people with no money who buy animal food in the grocery store to eat. Freddy bangs the bag of cat food against the floor and calls: Meow!

That's enough, Frederick.

He totters to his feet, then runs to her, hangs on her leg, rubs against her leg, pats her leg, wipes his mouth on her leg.

Freddy will live. Kim would be laughing her ass off at them, Stefanja and Lai Fun, the big nerds snared in the melodrama of motherhood, marriage, and adultery.

How did you hear? she asks Stefanja. What kind of cancer? How long was she sick?

Lai Fun puts Freddy down beside Olivia. Their sticky hands grab at each other, reminding her of herself and Thor. Lai Fun doesn't like to be reminded of herself and Thor when she in Stefanja's kitchen. Lai Fun fills the tea kettle with cold water and plugs it in.

Lloyd Weaselhead phoned me, Stefanja says. She bounces methodically on an exercise ball while she talks, her upper lip glossy with tears and snot. Lai Fun can't understand all the tears, all the snot, why Stefanja refuses to use the paper towel, how Stefanja can still bounce while obviously devastated.

I didn't even know she was sick, says Stefanja, bouncing and bouncing and crying and crying. That's so terrible. We didn't even know she was sick.

Lloyd Weaselhead and Kim were friends?

I was her friend. How come *I* didn't even know she was sick?

High school was twenty years ago, Stefanja.

Freddy stamps on an ant. Olivia punches Stefanja's exercise ball.

This is so bad, says Stefanja, stroking Olivia's hair, wiping Olivia's face with the paper towel. This is shitty and bad. I didn't even know she was sick. Who else is dying and I don't know it? Thank God Lloyd called me. At least we can go to the funeral, Lai Fun. Maybe other people from high school will be at the funeral. Maybe it'll be like a mini-reunion. That would be nice. Kim would like that.

Lai Fun is pretty sure Kim would *not* like a reunion held

around her coffin. She's starting to remember. Kim was expelled two months before graduation and didn't go to the end of year dance, which blew Lai Fun away because everyone wanted to go to the dance, why wouldn't you want to go to the end of year, end of Grade Twelve dance? Even though Lai Fun hated high school with every molecule in her body, she still went to the dance. Probably the last thing Kim would want is a reunion of the school that had expelled her, thrown around her bones. But funerals are good. So are weddings. So are end-of-year dances. They give closure.

Our school was such a disconnected, unhappy place, says Stefanja. She lays back on the ball and spreads her arms, her legs. She sucks up snot and wipes her nose with the back of her hand. The people who went to our school were sad and disoriented and are probably still unhappy in their little disconnected worlds. Here it is, almost twenty years since we graduated, and there's no twenty-year reunion organized that I've heard of, just like there was no ten-year reunion, just like there won't be a thirty-year reunion – Olivia, don't pinch – we'll all be dead and it will be like we sprang fully-grown from our mothers' heads – no childhoods, no history, no babies, no connection.

Our school was so fucking stupid! says Lai Fun. Bunch of apathetic losers. We went to school with those losers for twelve years! I'll bet none of them even speak French any more. I don't speak French any more, merci beaucoup.

It doesn't matter! says Stefanja. She flops onto her stomach and rolls herself toward the fridge. We should all still be in contact with each other! We should know if one of us is dying!

We'll go to the funeral, says Lai Fun, tucking her T-shirt back into her pants along with some more guilt. When is it?

Lloyd called me. I should call him back and help him call people.

Lai Fun hears the screech of the screen door on the back of the house. Thor.

35

I have to go home and give Freddy his dinner, Lai Fun says, grabbing her boy. When you've called Lloyd, call me and tell me when the funeral is.

She's down the back porch and halfway through the backyard.

The cat food! Stefanja shouts.

And we'll go have that reunion wake! Lai Fun shouts back from her front porch. Call me, Stefanja, okay?

Okay!

The rattle of the doorknob, a knocking on the back door, the migraine of the doorbell: Stef, I don't have my key! Thor says through the closed door.

Don't forget to call me, Stefanja, Lai Fun yells.

Who locked it? asks Stefanja. I didn't lock it. Don't go dying and not telling me, Lai Fun! she calls.

And Lai Fun runs back to Stefanja, Freddy still in her arms, and hugs Stefanja hard, their noses in each other's hair, their arms around each other tight tight, her best best friend since high school. Best friends forever. This is what Lai Fun would have written in Stefanja's yearbook – if Stefanja had asked Lai Fun to sign her yearbook. Which she never did. They weren't friends until second year university. Commerce 201.

Stef! calls Thor, rattling.

Lai Fun lifts Freddy on her shoulders, Olivia screaming in the house, Freddy yanked away from Olivia's plush purple rabbit family and squirrels, from his mother's shameful lust.

Meow! Freddy says. Sssssssssssss.

Lai Fun leaps across the lawn to her house, Freddy's kitten claws firmly in her fist. She fumbles with the key in one hand, her son in the other, she fumbles open the door and races into the house, a track-and-field baby obstacle course and she's forgotten the cat food and the water she set to boil in Stefanja's kettle. Wings of an eagle. Hind end of a lion. Griffins pulverized into the dust they came from.

Griffins on the bridge. She chews her fingernails. She was dreaming a regular, boring dream about putting on some lipstick when the griffins showed up offering her makeup advice – that colour makes your skin too orange, they said – even though the City Council took them down almost two years ago, even though she has no idea what happened to them after they decorated the bar at her wedding. She can't remember if she ever finished her letter to the City Council, but what does it matter – there are more important things than saving stone monsters in the downtown core. Her mother never sent a letter either, it turns out – too busy painting letters on signs to protest the demolition of the General Hospital, which the government imploded in a giant flower of forgotten asbestos and viruses and concrete and brick dust anyway. Lai Fun loves Jennifer. They have been together for six years, married for one and a half – her longest relationship ever – even though in her mind they were married the day they moved in together, the day she hauled her stuff to Jennifer's apartment and placed a vase of pink silk tulips in the middle of the kitchen table and her tool box in the hallway cupboard. That was enough for Jennifer, but these official dates are significant for Lai Fun. Being official and recognized is important, those matching rings on their marriage fingers mean they belong to one another, just like Freddy and the fetus belong to her.

Lai Fun is pregnant again. Jennifer comes home at ten PM, puts on her pyjamas, and wolfs down a grilled Tofurella sandwich. Later that night, she touches Lai Fun's tight stomach and talks to it, asks the fetus if she should use stripped, investment-grade bonds as a foundation for her portfolio or some other kind. Jennifer and Lai Fun laugh at Lai Fun's belches. In pink-bummed baboon lust Lai Fun kisses Jennifer on the lips, then Jennifer reaches over and turns out the light and once again Lai Fun is expected to cope with her horniness by rubbing up against the bedroom door-knob or something. She wants to yowl like an alley-cat, screw like a howler-monkey, fuck everything in sight. She lifts herself up from the bed, tip-toes to the den, and shoots Thor an email. Her skin screams in the night. She dreams about door-knobs.

Mornings before she goes to work, Jennifer brings Lai Fun and the fetus a nice cup of herbal tea and sets it on the bedside table. She lets Lai Fun doze while she drinks her coffee and gazes out the window at the silent, orderly houses that line the street, their house the biggest and most orderly of all. The cat swirls around Jennifer's feet, licking her with its long tail, as she prepares herself and the baby boy for the day. She gives Freddy his breakfast spoon by spoon, bites a grape in two and keeps one half in her mouth, holds the other half in front of Freddy's mouth. Good morning, Tweetie, she whispers, and Freddy blinks at her, then opens his mouth wide like a baby bird's. Chew chew, she says and she moves her jaw up and down and he moves his jaw up and down. She gives him his sippy-cup and says, Good morning, Puppy-man, and he growls until she whisper-laughs. She takes a sip of her coffee. He shrieks, then bangs his cup and milk sprinkles her hair, her eye-lashes.

At least this is what Jennifer used to do until Lai Fun's older sister Angélique – back from Montréal – moved into the basement and said she could give Freddy his breakfast and babysit when they needed her to. Now, Jennifer is at work before any of the other directors, the office staff. She sits in her office in front of her computer, and from her window she can see the sun roll across the sky. She brings in more and more money for the company and her baby and her wife and their perfect house. She will be a VP of Gargoyle Communications before the year is out. They will be rolling and kicking and giving birth in all the dough.

Lai Fun in bed, only ready to rise from the dead after Jennifer brings Freddy into the bedroom and then disappears with a soft key-click out the front door. Goodbye. A bientôt.

Lai Fun knows things will get better when the new baby comes and now that Angélique can be their nanny. They will get their Sundays and the occasional evening back. They will go out to Buddha's Veggie Delight instead of ordering in. They will talk about their work and politics and how the far right is taking over the country. They will spend time *not* talking about Freddy's new love of pointing bananas like they're guns, about how he's using his fingernails to get his way at play school, about how letting him lick the cat is not good for his physical health, although good for his emotional health they suppose, until the new baby comes. They can talk about things besides ear infections and car seats, they can swear and talk about the business section and have sex on top of the business section. They can have real fights about their stagnating relationship. Instead of using the warning word, "Gerbera," to signal that now is not the time for fighting, now is time for talking about how people and animals can fly when they don't have wings, Lai Fun will tell Jennifer that she is a shitty, neglectful spouse, merci beaucoup.

Nice dust bunny, er, dust hippo, says Lai Fun, pointing to the gap between the fridge and the cupboard. I don't think you've touched that vacuum since I bought it three months ago.

Gerbera, says Jennifer.

Does cows have wings? asks Freddy.

No, says Jennifer.

Gerbera! says Lai Fun.

I don't know, says Angélique who now joins them Saturday mornings for breakfast (Who the hell asked her? thinks Lai Fun). I saw a cow with wings just yesterday at the café, says Angélique.

She licks her finger and rubs Freddy's chin. Lai Fun didn't even see dirt on his chin.

I guess they would have been very big wings, says Lai Fun. She tightens one of the curls on Freddy's head with her index finger.

Very big, Jennifer says. Gerbera yourself.

Bigger than griffin wings, says Lai Fun.

Honey, says Jennifer, they have wings of stone.

There is no funeral service, Lloyd Weaselhead tells Stefanja over the phone. Kim didn't want one. Didn't even ask for donations to the cancer society or the SPCA or the Avalanche Victims' Help Fund, her Aunt Mariko says.

Kim liked to ski the back country? asks Lloyd.

No, says Aunt Mariko. Kim hated snow. Hated winter. Hated the fact that winter in Alberta is ten months long.

She draws in a wheezy, cigarette-tinged breath.

If we're lucky, she coughs. She coughs and hacks away phlegm in her throat.

See? says Stefanja to Lai Fun, I didn't even know that! We went to school with her for twelve years and we didn't even know that Kim hated snow. The things you learn about your best friends when you think you know everything there is to know about them.

I don't like snow, says Lai Fun.

Does Lloyd Weaselhead hate snow? I don't know! cries Stefanja. She fast-forwards through the *Let's Do Yoga!* tape to the head-stand. She places her head on the floor and stretches her legs up the wall.

Flute music, waterfalls, and the *Let's Do Yoga!* yogini in her bright red leotard sing-songing about lining up the chakras.

Everyone hates snow, says Lai Fun, aimlessly dangling a catnip ball in front of Freddy and Olivia. They start to whine. No one likes snow, says Lai Fun. We only like chinooks. My turn to do a head-stand, says Lai Fun.

Stefanja lowers her feet to the ground, bounces up. She grabs Freddy and Olivia by the hands and takes them to the kitchen for apple juice. Lai Fun rewinds the tape to the beginning of the head-stand, puts her head on the floor next to the wall. She takes a breath, takes a breath deep into her heart chakra. She can see clear across the room: underneath the sofa, the coffee table, the side-board. She sees a ball of blond Thor hair looking at her from across the room and she wants to throw up. She lifts up one leg. She breathes into each and every vertebra in her spine. She thinks about waterfalls and loose bladders.

I think we should plan the twenty-year reunion, calls Stefanja from the kitchen. We need to all be together. Be with our pack again. I want to know who's made their first million, had their seventh kid, who's living in a cardboard box in France; we're getting older and older, Lai Fun, and the reunions never happen. We'll have to plan one. I'll ask Lloyd Weaselhead if he wants to help. He managed to track down at least ten people for Kim's funeral-that-never-was. We'll do it. We'll crack this thing together and knock their hats off! Finally a reunion! I love parties!

Stefanja's naked feet pad out of the kitchen, along with Freddy and Olivia's tinier ones. Lai Fun looks at their feet, them standing around her, the way the toe pads on the three pairs of feet suction to the bare floor, the hairs and food crumbs and fingernail clippings and dust. She lifts both her legs up the wall. Lai Fun feels the blood and heat rush to her head, her horror and deception tipping out and flooding all over the floor.

Of course I'll help, she says, her face red and shining. It's not right that she's fucking Thor.

Let's Do Yoga! their Monday afternoon ritual. Stefanja her best and only friend. Later they will *Do Groceries!*

I got an email from Maddie, says Jennifer on a rare evening she's home before nine. She and Helen are breaking up. Isn't that awful? Twenty-three years down the tubes.

Did Maddie cheat on Helen? I knew it! Lai Fun is paging

through the high school yearbook. She's gotten to the D's. She looks at Stefanja's big hair and braces.

No, Maddie's found religion and Helen can't take it. We're never going to end. We'll be together for seventy-five years. I never managed to do the recycling. Did you?

Gerbera! Lai Fun nearly yells.

He's in bed, don't gerbera me.

When would I have had a chance to take in the recycling? asks Lai Fun. When I was buried under files at work this morning? Or when Freddy and I were waiting around for the fucking plumber to stop the water from pouring out underneath the sink this afternoon when I promised I'd baby-sit Olivia too?

I'm just asking, says Jennifer. The pile's just getting really high is all.

No, I didn't do the frigging recycling. You do the recycling! You don't do anything.

Recycling's *your* job. I'm going to bed.

Maybe when you're done sleeping, you could do a load of recycling.

Whatever, says Jennifer.

Lai Fun cries in the bathtub because the bathtub is her favourite place to cry, so clean and orderly, the water from her eyes, in the tub, on her skin, soaked into her pores, splashed in her hair, and she can say that the reason her eyes are so red is because she got soap-water in them.

She steps out of the tub, dries herself off and climbs into bed. Surprise. Jennifer is asleep so Lai Fun doesn't have to explain her swollen, blood-shot eyes.

That night, she dreams she's flattening empty tin cans for recycling with her bare feet.

CHAPTER 2

Louve wears the red patent leather boots with the pointy toes and stiletto heels. On sale, seventy-five percent off. Running shoes in her bag because she had to take them home to wash. In her bag along with her cigarettes, her lipstick in the silvery leather case she bought in the 1960s but still holding up just fine, Kleenex, compact, calendar, lighter, gum, lucky rabbit's knuckles. She carefully click-clacks through the slush across the street to the bus shelter. Her boots are not very snow-worthy, but quite striking against the grey of the street, the grey of the falling snow in the street light. Beautiful and appropriate to her mood.

Good morning, Serge! she calls to the bus driver, even though it's night-time, even though it's always night-time when she says good morning to Serge Butot the bus driver – night-shift people like her have a strange sense of humour and time and sleep patterns. He says to her, Nice coat, and she says, I'm happily married you know, because sometimes his flirting goes a little overboard. Even though tonight she is not quite so happily married, having had a fight with Fritz-Peter about the joint chequing account. The joint chequing account is ruining their marriage just like the joint savings account did last year. She had had *enough* when he said he wanted to buy cowboy boots, no sale price, and that there was money in the chequing account last time he looked. Like they can afford flittery cowboy boots with her pension and his gas station job, although sometimes Lai Fun gives them money, which Louve hates, but it is a relief every so often to have an extra shot of money to cover the bills. But not a cowboy boot bill. She blows her nose. The two hundred and fifty dollars Lai Fun gave them is not for cowboy boots. Louve hoped it could sit in the joint chequing for longer than a week, because Fritz-Peter hardly ever remembers the joint chequing.

Fritz-Peter never used to care about cowboy boots. She opens her lipstick case, checks her lipstick, bares her teeth in the dim light of the bus because she had to put her lipstick on in such a hurry. Her lips bright; she fingertips away a glob from her left incisor, her teeth shiny and healthy strictly because of genetics, because they can no longer afford the dentist. All the better to eat her husband with. Their marriage was practically in the toilet because of cowboy boots, footwear Fritz-Peter had nothing but contempt for when they first moved here. Now he thinks they're sexy, so sexy and perfect he needs them and would sooner give up his marriage than those snakeskin pointed toes. Is there another woman maybe? A secret drug addiction? Louve would like to know.

Just sometimes they are a little too near the *edge*. Living one too many dollars beyond their means, like when Fritz-Peter suddenly needs to buy boots and the boots aren't even on sale. Relying on her babies is not how Louve wants to picture her graceful ascent into the golden years.

But Mama, says Lai Fun, Jennifer and I make more than enough between us.

You should put it away for yourselves. For the baby.

And Lai Fun tut-tuts, slips the cheque into her mother's

coat pocket, or leaves it hidden inside the breadbox.

Her eldest daughter Angélique's cheques once appeared in the mail. No letter, just a cheque made out to Louve. These cheques have stopped now that Angélique has lost her job, moved cities, lives in her sister's basement.

Louve hasn't said anything to Angélique. Angélique inclined to dress in black since she moved back west, like she is a widow or a starving artist. Probably a broken love affair because Angélique has always gone for the dramatic, but how would Louve know? God forbid Angélique would tell her own *mother* about her life. Louve didn't even know Angélique was gay until Lai Fun told her.

Don't be stupid, Mama! Lai Fun said. Just *look* at her. It's so obvious.

Obvious to you, said Louve. I'm not *psychic*.

The bus stops on the bridge. The bus always stops on the bridge. Four minutes, it waits above the water, right next to the grown-over scars of the missing griffins. Louve hopes their poor, cracked, mixed-up bodies ended up in a nice cemetery, not just in Hotel Macdonald's dusty basement, or dumped in a ravine. Here the bus sits. Right in view of the other scar, this one covered by shiny new condos and a strip mall and a ritzy community hall. The site of the demolished General Hospital, but luckily there is no moon tonight so Louve doesn't have to see.

She finally told Fritz-Peter to shut his cake-hole (she has no idea where this phrase came from, probably her teenage-boy colleagues at work, it just popped out). Fritz-Peter shut his cake-hole immediately and now Louve feels like a rotten wife and if Fritz-Peter up and leaves her, well, she shouldn't be surprised. After she told him to shut his cake-hole, she marched into the kitchen, sat down at the table, and began to put her face on while she drank her Nabob coffee, ate a Tofurkey leg whole without a single chew because she was starving, and smoked a cigarette. She finished her lipstick last: made sure there was no Tofurkey grease on her mouth, then quickly lined and spread the crimson around her own cake-hole. She put the clean white runners in her battered leather bag. She chose the red boots because they are the same colour as her lipstick, as the petals of her roses, that velvet-red hue that once made her happy even though her roses are buried under the snow, still makes her happy, even though she's just told her husband to shut up, that is too stupid to live, and how he finds his way out of bed in the mornings is beyond her comprehension. Even though she paid for the red boots out of her own account, not the joint account, he will never understand that joint accounts are for groceries or electric bills. The newspaper subscription.

She can picture him sitting straight-backed as ever at the kitchen table, spreading his resentment on crackers and stuffing them whole into his cake-hole. Her nightshift job fixing airplane upholstery and cargo netting in Furnishings is boring enough without her being paranoid about her husband too. Cowboy boots. She is not working this part-time job in addition to getting her pension so that he can play at being Johnny Cash. Or Leonard Cohen.

She sits on Serge Butot's bus and smudges the toes of her hot red boots in the melted snow and gravel soup on the bus floor. Poor Serge Butot, he was just trying to be nice, what's wrong with a little flirtation, and her coat *is* very nice – a trench coat with a tiger print pattern she got on sale sixteen years ago. She looks down at her red boots and feels the pinch in the bones of her feet, especially the right one, because frankly, her feet are a mess from so many years being a nurse. But this shouldn't mean that she can't occasionally wear nice boots, should it, especially since she still has the legs and her boots set off her calves so very well.

Her feet may be wrecked, but Louve believes it's all the walking she's done in her nurse life that's made her legs so ridiculously shapely. Walking to the hospital, walking in the hospital, walking from the hospital, not to mention the other jobs she's had. Now she has to take a bus to a job where she sits for twelve hours while her calves wobble at best, and the only thing walking is her fingers on sewing machines while she listens to the dirty jokes and masturbatory whinings of the twenty-three-year-old cake-holes around her. Which is why she has started jogging during the midnight lunch break. She started jogging to get away from the hospital's screams the day the government imploded it, the giant dust plumes, the crack, the crumble, the crush, and the final fall of the geriatric building; snide remarks about tits.

Serge Butot lurches the bus forward, almost giving her whiplash. When the bus gets to her stop, Louve steps off on her shapely legs and totters carefully toward the hangar in her fire engine red boots.

CHAPTER 3

Lai Fun paces the school hallways in her long suede coat, her water-proof, polished leather boots with the big ol' heels, black leather gloves, while she waits for Stefanja. All gifts from Louve. She would never buy leather, but she feels tall and beautiful and important dressed up in the leather. She is not the loser she was when she had to go to this stupid sandstone building every day or else get thrown in jail or a foster home. She is muscular, smooth, and smart-looking in her glasses, her single, long braid. She is five-foot-five in her heels instead of five-foot-two. She is tall, gorgeous, and gay. Back in high school she was an asexual amoeba. She looks at her watch. She has until 12:45 and then home to Freddy. Time has atrophied the hallways into concrete tunnels, the air close and stiff, the gymnasium still smells of rubber and Phys Ed panic. She strides into the cafeteria: big black-and-white tiles checker the floor, new glass doors that open onto the interior courtyard. A floor, a courtyard, and doors too nice for a hell-hole high school. She looks out the window, turns back to the room.

A television monitor up near the ceiling shows the cafeteria empty except for herself and a clump of three students. Perhaps she is on some security guard's screen right now.

Yes, this school's definitely shrunk and she's grown. The football field smaller, the fences around the school property shorter. The teacher's parking lot where she used to get big erections from staring at the football players is a tiny concrete square. She wasn't gay then. She fell for boys all the time. Smelled boys, looked at their skin, their hair, their fingers, their necks, their hidden genitals. She looked at them and wanted them or tried to want them in her mouth, on top of her. What she would do with them once they were there she wasn't sure, but it was the thing to want. Boys. Boys.

She wasn't gay then. Although she was always gay – gay from the second she was born – she just got swept up in the other girls' hysteria.

A teacher taps by in lab coat and princess heels. A particular outside corner of the building smells like dry-cleaning, like her wife. She's finally free to be gay and tall (only those slutty headbanger girls wore three-inch heels in high school) and here she is, screwing her next-door neighbour Thor, a fucking *boy*. She clicks around the floor in a sloppy figure eight, hitting her heels down hard, her hands in her coat pockets. But Thor doesn't count. If she were sleeping with a woman, then it would count, then she would be a regular adulteress instead of just some neglected same-sex wife.

Yes, she was utterly gay then, but it was too difficult in school. And how could she realize when everyone *told* her she was supposed to want boys' cocks in her mouth and between her legs? She dutifully loved boys, lived them, and died them, from the shoulders up. Louve would ask her, Did you let that boy touch you? and Lai Fun would know that she should have asked that boy to touch her, why didn't that boy want to touch her? Boys. While her heart tangled in the messy crush of Hadley Constable's curls. Preppy Hadley Constable's pearls. All those preppy girls in their pearls and braces and crisp shirts.

49

Too young to be gay. Too good to be gay. Too short to be gay. Secret best friends with Lloyd Weaselhead – the closeted singing football player.

Stefanja has forced her into this and the pit of Lai Fun's stomach twists like some dead fish in an abandoned aquarium. She'd like to sprout wings, a lion's powerful haunches, and spring up and away. Lai Fun swore when she left this place she would never come back. She faced straight ahead when she walked out the school's front doors for the last time in June 1985; eyes on the road, moving away from the sandstone face of that fucking school.

Stefanja practically begged Lai Fun to help with the reunion, begged so hard Lai Fun didn't have the heart to say, But you hardly spoke to me until Commerce 201 in university.

Lai Fun doesn't want to imagine what Stefanja will do when she finds out she's remembered Lai Fun all wrong.

Lai Fun closes her eyes. Picks up and twists the pearls from around Hadley's neck. Holds the strands up and dangles them from the ceiling. Strands of pearls swinging, long, delicate ropes. Green and white balloons – the stupid school's stupid colours – cluster the ceiling like ants' eggs, like genetically modified grapes; the walls, the streamers, paper flowers, banners. At the centre of each table an apple and a ruler, or an apple and a map, something cute like that. The cafeteria because the gymnasium would be completely unacceptable with its stench of sneaker rubber and basketball sweat and Social Dance 20 humiliation.

A bar by the courtyard doors. Yes. A martini fountain because everyone will need a fuck-load of drinks and there are always drinks at ceremonies like this. They will bring food in – it must happen here in the cafeteria, the only half-decent room in the school, otherwise she will not participate in the travesty. She opens her eyes. A live band on the raised platform. A small gift for everyone who attends. A small sack of flower seeds with a poem attached? A page from the dictionary rolled and tied with a ribbon?

Bad news! Stefanja calls. Lai Fun looks at the monitor and sees Stefanja walk toward her. They look like two middle-aged women, overdressed, pacing in their old high school cafeteria. Is she middle-aged? No. But Stefanja is, definitely. They stand in a french fry and potato chip miasma. Their stiff clothes, their confidence make them look like parents, not students.

She will arrange their graduation photos along the walls of the cafeteria. A bagpiper to open the party, who will slowly walk through the doors by the Coke machine and through the cafeteria all the way to the door leading to the hallway by the Principal's office. Jennifer will know where to find a bagpiper. Maybe a bagpiper *trio*.

They weren't very helpful, which is surprising, says Stefanja. She paws through her purse and takes out one of her gloves. They said because of confidentiality they couldn't release addresses or telephone numbers. They told me to use the names in the yearbook and look them up in the phone book. What a shame. Otherwise they were very nice. Remember the secretary with the red hair, Mrs Beadle? She's a real sweetie. Has twelve grandchildren now. Hair still ketchup red.

She wipes her nose with the glove.

You should have mentioned you're not some kind of fucking stalker and that you just want to show your fucking Trojan pride, says Lai Fun. That's what you should have said.

It will just be our pet project. Like in the old days when we worked backstage on the school production of *The Mikado*, remember? Remember what a riot that was? Good times!

Lai Fun stares at Stefanja dabbing her nose and buttoning up her coat. Stefanja's memory holey as lace.

Torches in the courtyard. Lai Fun's saved wedding decorations. She loved figuring out the menu for her wedding with Jennifer and explaining to the hotel chef exactly what vegan meant and what vegan didn't mean. She loved Jennifer ordering her to phone caterers and hotels, loved driving down to fabric stores and dress stores and running her hands over the brocades and raw silks and combination polyester-cottons of tablecloths and dresses and shawls and dress shirts. She loved meeting with the baker three times to argue about the cake, figuring out how to cope with the fact that she'd gained pregnancy weight in her ass and didn't fit her skirt any more. She loved the precise rows of sparkling glasses and cutlery and bundles of flowers and ribbons and silver paper and gold balloons when she and Jennifer and her mother and Stefanja double-checked the ballroom just before the reception. Loved the chandeliers and the ceiling in that ballroom, everything there for her and Jennifer. So why does her stomach feel like she's swallowed a cockroach when she thinks about planning a high school reunion?

Now we just have to raise money, says Stefanja. We have to book a place. Make a lot of phone calls. That'll be *fun*! Catching up on old times.

I want to hold the reunion here in the school cafeteria, Lai Fun says.

Only fifteen minutes left before she has to go home to Freddy. She and Stefanja look at the graduation photos lining the hallways. Kim of course not on the walls because she was expelled. Mrs Blake's fault. Stefanja back when she was a gel-permed brunette instead of a silvery-streaked, sleek blonde. Hadley Constable, that preppy judge's kid, in her pouffy taffeta gown at the graduation dance, boys trailing her because she could talk them into thinking they were sexy, because her dad was rich, because she lived in a giant house in Eagle Ridge with her other cake-faced siblings. All the Constable kids would be lawyers, judges one day. It was programmed into their genetic codes. Hadley Constable! Holy shit! Lloyd Weaselhead. Popular just like Hadley even though Lloyd didn't live in a big house, even though no one knew where Lloyd lived, *because* no one knew where Lloyd lived, not his pretend-girlfriends, not even his best friend Mike Paperny. Lloyd Weaselhead, the famous singing football player. Who turned on Lai Fun. His one true friend.

Also they're going to blow up the school, says Stefanja, stepping on Lai Fun's heels. It's scheduled for demolition in two years. That's the saddest thing. I'm going to write a letter. I'm sure this building is a heritage site of some sort. Maybe we could have our reunion *and* save the building too!

CHAPTER 4

Louve watches the implosion from the roof of another nurse's monster-sized station wagon on a hill north of the hospital. Fritz-Peter calls in sick that day, and Louve drinks litres of Nabob so she will stay awake, then she and Fritz-Peter walk to the hill to watch with the crowds. She doesn't want to go, but she knows if she doesn't it will be like missing a funeral. She needs the ceremony and the ritual of seeing the dead body so she can believe it and grieve. Louve carries the six-pack of beer in an old canvas backpack of Fritz-Peter's. Fritz-Peter straps the lawn chairs to his back, and normally Louve would laugh because he looks so silly, but she doesn't because today is a funeral. Fritz-Peter and Louve join the ex-patients, nurses, doctors, housekeeping staff parked on the hill overlooking the General Hospital. They share their beer even though it is 8:30 in the morning and sit in the chairs until there are too many people blocking their view and they have to sit on Arden's, the other nurse's, giant American car, and Louve wishes she brought her hat because the wind and the sun are deep-frying the ends of her hair.

Arden crouches down to take pictures, but complains because she can't take in the whole building *and* the smoke-stack.

She would have brought the video camera, but couldn't find it at the last minute. Arden complains that she really needs a bourbon, but she says okay to one of the beers. She clicks her camera at various dismembered parts of the building trying to get a panorama: the front door, the smoke-stack, the newer addition. But the windows are sledgehammered in, the whole hospital fenced in with security guards to keep people out. A security guard saunters around the parking lot where Fritz-Peter used to come pick Louve up at the end of a nightshift to walk her home and the commissionaire would give Fritz-Peter hell for loitering in the emergency zone.

The papers and the newscasts say the neighbourhood is quarantined.

A man rubs the old scar and new stitches in the centre of his chest and sits with his binoculars. All the government's fault, he says.

No, says Fritz-Peter. It's the bastards in City Hall. Doing their municipal mafia duty.

The nurses burning out and patients dying from negligence, the teachers with full-to-bursting classrooms, now imploding hospitals. The government adorns itself with cutbacks like jewellery.

The government pushes over the decrepit downtown hospital even though no voters said yes, and as the building implodes, Arden stops complaining and Louve feels the hot ocean in her eyes and the man with the stitches takes the binoculars away from his face. The walls are insulated with ancient bacteria and viruses, the ghosts of sick and dying patients and the people who worked there. Agony palpable in the mushroom-cloud of dust from the contracting building.

When they blow up Louve's hospital, they blow up her life. This parking lot is where her youngest daughter was born, she says, when the rubble is cleared away. This brand-new drug store or new condo development or pile of unresolved dirt you're pissing on is the same spot my husband had his hernia fixed, she says. Now there's only a ghost of a hospital. For a while the city sells off the bricks one by one as souvenirs. For a while she has a brick with its clinging chunks of mortar on the gas-fire mantelpiece they never turn on, but then she takes it down and mingles it with all the other ornamental bricks in the bed in the garden plot she rents from the city for twenty-five dollars a year. She can't remember which brick it is any more.

After years of piles of dirt, weeds, and wire fencing, they put in a new condo development, a strip mall, a drive-through burger joint, and a sports bar on the old hospital block and Louve knows that this is a desecration. Like building a strip club on the bones of a family member. When she walks too near the hospital ghost, her hands start to stink of blood and bleach.

Not that the hospital was ghost-free when it was still standing. She remembers faucets turning on by themselves, cold spots right around the bed of the coma patient who died alone while his family haggled over his possessions. Patients screaming because they saw a nun in full habit standing over them in the bed. Blowing up the building is sacrilege, it unburies the dead and their personal effects.

Just a brick, but a brick imprinted with the drama of the building: the patients, the phlebotomists, the nutritionists, the house-keepers, the porters, the commissionaires, the ladies in the flower-shop. The nurses and the doctors – blood and vomit and shit and bile.

For Louve, being a nurse was not a choice: it was an overwhelming compulsion. Why else stick around to do such a godforsaken job scrubbing out people's asses, wrestling with 400-pound comatose bodies to the point that Louve ruins her own spine, her shoulders, her wrists, and her feet for hardly any money and no sympathy?

Louve smoked next to the doors opening on to the morgue, which was the only place in the hospital where smoking was allowed. The dead don't breathe. Nurses and doctors, especially nurses, the worst chain smokers of all – they hung out with the cops and the paramedics. This is why so many nurses marry cops, the smoking bond, the emergency unit bond, the bond of new corpses chauffeured in the giant doors.

Didn't matter how may tracheotomies she inserted, cleaned, and re-adjusted, the bloody hacking of emphysema patients. Louve smokes too much, she burned out long ago, her lungs like her hospital with its punctured windows, the smoke-stack puffing out smoke from incinerated limbs, chunks of cancer, redundant antibiotics.

Louve hears about the demolition from Fritz-Peter, of course. On slow nights at the gas station he reads *The Globe and Mail*, *The Guardian*, *Weekly World News*, and *The Journal* straight through, no interruptions.

They're closing down the General Hospital, Fritz-Peter says. Did they mention it at work? Where will you be transferred?

No. I don't know. Who's closing it down? The city? Why?

The government. Going to demolish it. To save money. Hitler's hiding on the moon, too. Says so in the *Weekly*. Terrible they didn't mention it to you.

Fritz-Peter holds the lighter under Louve's heart with his words and walks away to watch *I Love Lucy* reruns when the heart begins to smoulder. Louve walks home alone after work because Fritz-Peter had an evening shift at the gas station – he the only employee calm enough to talk his way out of the constant hold-ups.

The giant dust plumes, the crack, the crumble, the crush, and the screams of the hospital's gargoyles as they thump to the ground and shatter. When the government blows up the hospital, violently puts the gargoyles to sleep, they cauterize Louve's compulsion. As she and Fritz-Peter lumber back home through the clouds of dust and grief, she realizes that what she thought was her calling was nothing but a perverted love for a virus-soaked building built in the fifties. Funny, that. But she still mourns the object of her affection.

She assumes they will transfer her to the new hospital on the other side of the city with all the other nurses on her ward – she maps out the bus route and frets about perfect bus times. But they ask her – no, *tell* her – to retire instead. They throw her into the fire with the rest of the deadwood and for the last weeks she goes to work and tends to the patients as she normally would – she calmly administers drugs and injections, changes bloodied diapers, checks pulses, monitors the fluids that go in and out, reassures and restrains the dying and the dead. She does her job the way she has done it for years and years, but on her breaks, on her walks to and from work – twenty-eight more work days, twenty-seven, twenty-six – she cannot catch her breath, she cannot stop the trembling and the freezing in her viscera.

We will find a way, says Fritz-Peter into her neck, his arms bundling together her rib-cage and elbows and knuckles and drooping skull.

She will tend her garden. Unfold the roses and leafy greens in her garden patch rented from the city, she and Fritz-Peter will crochet baby berets and jackets, she will sew upholstery and cargo nets for her nephew's airline even though she stopped speaking to his mother years ago. She will thaw her insides by jogging regularly, she will become a writer. She has always had a novel inside her as she has led a mostly interesting life; she has a suitcase full of diaries in the storage area of their apartment building. She doesn't need the hospital. She believes she can do anything. Write a book. Become a marathon runner. She can throw over her addiction.

On her last shift, while she is labelling and packing lamps and iv poles, her last patient is dying. A ninety-year-old man with Alzheimer's named Joe who swears in Ukrainian.

He drums the windowsill with his fists.

What's wrong, Joe?

He drums and swears and points, but she doesn't know Ukrainian, she sees nothing obvious. He shakes his finger toward the window, but when she looks out, there's only an ambulance parked in the emergency zone.

He lays his brittle body back down onto the bed and stares at the invisible people patrolling his hallways.

Joe coughs up blood all night, his heart fizzes in and out, a weak radio signal. The Intensive Care Unit team rushes in with the crash-cart, but the drugs, the paddles, the extra oxygen cannot save him.

Louve mops up the blood from Joe's face, from his hair, from where it's pooled in the intricate bowls of his ears. The blood smears on her fingers and knuckles and wrists, gets in her mouth. She tongues the salt carefully.

She turns off the oxygen and the IV. She straightens out his body, closes his eyes, tucks his dentures back into his mouth. Bathes Joe's body with warm water from a basin, towels him off, rolls him back and forth as she changes the sheets under him, crosses his arms over his chest. She fills out the information on his tag, ties the tag around the toe. A fresh pillow under his head. She rolls up a towel and stuffs it under his chin to keep his mouth from falling open, pulls up the clean sheet and tucks it under his chin. She phones Joe's daughter, but only gets her voice-mail.

Last patient, last body, last day. Too poetic.

Louve might even go to Joe's funeral if the family invites her. He belonged to the hospital. She can tell from the way his fingers with their hard, cracked nails caressed the windowsill when he saluted the sun every morning from the window. The force of his hands as he squished his silent, shouting lips against the glass. The eagerness with which he pushed up his sleeves for the needle or the intravenous. His veins clear and jumping out of the skin on his arm.

Louve still gets aroused by the sight of a healthy vein, even though now she is officially in Furnishings at the airline and hardly ever comes into contact with veins any more. Big veins the diameter of night crawlers perfect for inserting a needle. She did not cry as she prepared Joe's body for presentation to his daughter. But Louve cries when she and Fritz-Peter see a dead body lying stiffly by the river behind yellow police tape on one of their walks home from the hospital. Or when she sees a dead cat sprawled next to the curb. Or a bee caught under a windshield wiper. Later she always retraces her steps and bundles up the cat, scrapes off the bee, buries them in her tiny garden.

Florence Nightingale died of syphilis. A little too ardent in her bedside care. On her last day of work, after Louve finishes zipping ninety-year-old Joe and his bald, worried head into his shroud, Louve washes her hands twice, applies lotion to them, fills out her report, puts on her coat, and prepares to walk home the long, difficult way through downtown.

D'you wanna go for a drink? asks another nurse.

It's seven in the morning! Louve protests.

We could go to my house. I have some Melba toast if you need to eat.

But Louve declines and walks through the smog of early traffic and the clicking of the traffic-lights. She walks over the Centre Street bridge, under the arches over the sidewalk, under the griffins busy staring at the city, staring at her; she walks past the Bay department store and sees an eel lying on the meridian where Centre Street meets Groat Road. The cold sun peeps out over the horizon and she nearly slips on the long, black eel, the length of an arm. Her hair blowing around and showing off the grey curly hair near the roots, the dead eel on the concrete meridian. As strange as if one of the griffins had followed her and when she turned around to look at it, pretended to wait for a streetcar.

60

She stares at the eel. She picks it up, puts it in her bag.

She walks past her desolate wintry garden patch on the way up to their apartment building. The frozen earth cracks, shifts, as she walks by.

Health care has gone to the dogs and it's all those politicians' fault. Pierre Trudeau would never have allowed this. Social spending ballooned during his term. Or no, he was tax cuts to the wealthy. He appreciated beautiful women and beautiful cities and this city makes a point of destroying all things beautiful. Trudeau – he was in a class by himself.

When they implode Louve's hospital and retire her and give her the pension which is not very much, but with Fritz-Peter working at the gas station is still enough to cover the rent and bills and an occasional Tuesday night movie or a play preview, Louve decides to write the novel that has always been inside her, and train for that marathon.

The hospital dipped her fingers into my heart, and wiped what she found there on her pant leg, writes Louve with her father's old pen on a brand new notepad from the Telstar Drug Mart. *"Breakfast!" the nurse shouts. Oh no, she thinks. The leeches have taken her literally.*

If she'd had a boy, Louve would have named him Marcel. She got to name the first daughter, Angélique, Fritz-Peter named Lai Fun, and now it's Louve's turn again. Louve has asked Lai Fun to name the baby Marcel. Or Marcelle – whichever the case. Frederick is named after a Prussian homosexual, isn't it Louve's turn? Always the homosexuality. Two daughters and both homosexuals. She cannot fathom how all this homosexuality came to be.

Luckily training for a marathon requires no machines, no fancy equipment, just motivation and a pair of working legs. Louve runs along the banks of the river in the dusk because the day's end is so much cooler, the path less busy. She shouts for Fritz-Peter to keep up on the bicycle he found in the alley by the gas station, the path paved, but crumbling and bumpy with the roots of trees, super-weeds, and lilac bushes in full bloom. The rubber of her thongs slaps the pavement – she will invest in a pair of on-sale runners if this first jog works – and soon she will have blisters between her toes, and her heels will crack from the repeated impact, the nub of the bone in her heel will drill through the tough flesh. The first jog of her life is a brilliant thing of pain.

My feet, Fritz-Peter!

Her hair sticks to her forehead, sweat pours over her scalp. Mascara and eyeliner pool around her eyes, collect in the folds between lid and eyebrow, her lipstick feathers. By now Fritz-Peter has ditched the bicycle. It was too small anyway – a little girl's with a long, pink banana seat and red plastic tassels hanging from the handle-bars. He lopes beside her in his socks and sandals, his hands full of lilacs he's ripped from the bushes lining the path.

Sweat smell dripping her armpits. She feels like a great, big, bouncing roast beef. The black T-shirt glued to her giant breasts; she holds one in each hand to stop the lurching. Her belly also bounces. Her buttocks. Her thighs, her calves. Her lungs bounce out of her mouth and she is sure she will die. Her tongue feels like it has been gutted and filleted.

One minute and fifty-four seconds.

Fritz-Peter lopes beside her; big, healthy veins in his arms, the diameter of a night crawler. In spite of the pain, Louve is aroused and curves off her jogging trajectory to a bench closer to the river. She is suddenly very glad she married Fritz-Peter and his over-sized veins. They watch the bats come out and spin past the lampposts. She kisses the insides of his elbows. Lays her heart against his chest and listens to his blood-song.

Later that night, Louve sits on her sore buttocks, puts her cracked feet up and writes: *Yes, my patient's tits terminated in dog's heads, but as a nurse, I'd seen everything.*

Perhaps she would leaf through another one of her gardening catalogues. Perhaps she would go fry up a sausage as an homage to the days before she became a vegetarian and then bury the sausage in her garden. Shut the windows and let the smell linger in the apartment.

In spite of the non-stop echoes of her hospital being imploded, it has been a very good day.

CHAPTER 5

October two years from now they will blow up the school. The carved blocks of sandstone, the stained-glass fans over the front entrance door, the carved wooden staircases inside. This tragic, beautiful building is the reason Lai Fun will plan the reunion, not because she has betrayed Stefanja and wants to balm her own guilt.

The doomed building, and the fact that her school never has reunions because everyone thinks reunions happen by themselves, just like office Christmas parties or non-denominational holiday receptions. People apparently believe reunions happen sort of like garbage collection, or shit flushing down the toilet to who-knows-where to be sifted through by who-knows-whom. Non-denominational office Holiday Receptions happen by themselves. You pay your fifty cents per paycheque into the social fund and God or Satan or the ghost of a secretary who loved her job so much she never went home whips together not only the booking of the hall, but the band, the blue and white non-denominational holiday decorations (snowflakes are okay, holly is iffy), the magically-materializing food. She sets up, takes down, rents the furniture and equipment, and has the

time and inclination and artistic eye to put together a very nice
8½ × 11 invitation to boot.

This is not to say that God, or most likely Satan, doesn't
sometimes also arrange reunions, like meeting your ex-husband
Alfred on a street corner in Madrid – Alfred who divorced your
ass so cruelly you cried your eyeballs out of their sockets for
eight years straight. Or when the long-lost twin sister named
Moira you never knew you had suddenly phones and insinu-
ates herself into your life and your children's lives, scrubs the
twelve years of soap-scum off the *top* of the bathroom shower
walls for god's sake, and around Christmas time asks for a little
cash, about five thousand should do it. Fate arranges reunions
of this kind all the time. But high school reunions? These take
super-secretary planning, commitment, co-ordination, and a
nostalgia so strong it physically compels like rotting chicken in
the garbage.

Lai Fun cannot rely on Fate to conjure the cosmic junc-
ture that will require the coincidence of every high school grad
of 1985 being in the same building at the same time wearing
their semi-best clothes and brightest faces. Fate has already had
twenty years and has pulled off not one single reunion. Lai Fun
with Stefanja's help will fine-tooth comb their yearbooks, they
will make the phone book their only lover. They will put messages up on the alumni website. They will send out psychic sig-
nals. They will put ads in newspapers because time is of the
essence, time is running out. They will phone ancient phone
numbers, new listings, visit friends of friends of friends, Google
the net for first names, last names, long-forgotten nicknames.
They will knock graduates up for money. It is May. They will
have the reunion in October. Lai Fun will be eight months pregnant. There's no better time. Last night, she dreamed she was
sitting on the toilet and peeing and that obviously means she
should go ahead with the reunion if she wants to sort out her
marriage unhappiness and her deteriorating maternal skills,

if she wants to save the antique building, keep her friendship with Stefanja, remember her place in the world as a good wife / mother / employee, of course that's what dreaming of peeing means.

We must have the reunion at the school, announces Lai Fun. In the cafeteria. She power-pushes Freddy's stroller in front of her, navigating the bumps and cracks as she power-marches.

We can't, says Stefanja. She pushes Olivia's stroller. She has weights strapped to her ankles to strengthen her quadriceps. She wanted to jog but Lai Fun said she needed a break, jogging makes her want to puke now that she's pregnant. When she double-checks to make sure the door is locked that night, Lai Fun will see Stefanja step out of her house in her sweats and run like a maniac up the street.

Why not?

Mrs Beadle said the school is all booked up in October for the International Choir Exchange Festival.

Oh well, says Lai Fun, puffing and sweating and puffing. I never really liked that cafeteria. All the dances were in there and no one ever asked me to dance so that would be too humiliating. You know what? I hated that entire building. It's fine as a museum piece, but I really don't want to spend more time there. That place is fucking haunted like my mother's old hospital. Haunted with Mr Kumar who breathed all over my fetal pig, Mrs Schneider who read my diary out loud to the whole class, Mr Moby who got his car fire-bombed and liked to hug all the good-looking girls too much. And it's too small.

And Mrs Blake, says Stefanja.

Brrr, says Lai Fun. Mrs Blake. I forgot about her.

I had my first marriage proposal in that cafeteria, says Stefanja.

Your *first*? How many have you had?

A few, murmurs Stefanja. We could have the reunion in a community hall.

I hate the ceilings in community halls! wails Lai Fun. They make me feel like I've been abducted and abandoned in a basement!

I'll start at the beginning of the names in the yearbook, Stefanja says, raising her knees even higher with each step, and work my way forward. You start from the end and work backward. We have to keep bugging Lloyd Weaselhead! He'll have phone numbers. You try phoning him again. He's just above Carol Zindel.

Lloyd Weaselhead. Lloyd Weaselhead, Lai Fun's once perfect secret friend, but now "Lloyd Weaselhead" makes her grind her teeth in her sleep so loud even Jennifer hears it and Lai Fun pretends she is asleep when Jennifer says, Honey, who are you gnashing up? Our baby? Put in your night-guard. I have to get up at five!

Like Lai Fun doesn't also have to get up at five. A thirty-eight-year-old woman wearing a night-guard in her mouth is too stupid for words!

Lloyd Weaselhead got to sing alone during ukulele class in grade one even though it was ukulele class and not even singing time. He sang at all the school assemblies, won all the talent shows. People knew he would be famous in spite of his being the cause of every fight in the schoolyard. But then Lloyd Weaselhead played his first football game and the singing gig was up because suddenly singing was for fags.

Fags?

Lloyd Weaselhead rams the quarterback with his giant football shoulders, wrestles him to the ground, kneels with his legs around the quarterback's ass, and when Lloyd Weaselhead takes off his helmet, out swings his thick, black, sweaty hair. Lloyd Weaselhead betrayed her, by denying what a big fag he is.

Lai Fun pulled Lloyd Weaselhead out of the closet with both hands. He grabbed onto clothes hooks, the bar for hanging clothes, finally the edges of the closet door, but she pulled

67

him out anyway, the operetta-singing football player who was so boy-gorgeous everyone forgot he wasn't even white and only she and Corby Knudsen knew he was gay and if she ever told anyone he was the football gig would be up, but she never did, she never did. Lloyd Weaselhead. She saved his fucking life.

She loved Lloyd Weaselhead in high school like he was her twin separated at birth, kept his secret identity in her hope-chest along with her *Maclean's Magazine* special issue on Lady Diana and Prince Charles's Royal Wedding, the *Maclean's* special issue on Nadia Comaneci, the naked rubber dolls her godmother gave her which she never played with but never threw away even when she turned sixteen, her diaries (all of them half-full except for the little, little one Fritz-Peter bought for her in Chinatown with the purple brocade cover which she filled right up, it fit so perfectly in her palm), dusty, crumbling seashells from a beach in Vancouver, and a plastic hat from New Year's, the one when she was allowed to drink half a glass of beer the night she called Lloyd Weaselhead at his house and said, I'm soooo drunk.

And he had to be nice to her, he had to because she knew he was gay and he knew she knew, so instead of hanging up on her he said, You've never been drunk before? What kind of space ship do you live in?

And in the hallway on the first day of school after Christmas holidays, she saw him hanging out with the cool guys in their tasseled leather shoes and the cool girls in their pearls and perfect asymmetrical haircuts and she said, I got drunk *again* the day after I called you.

Lloyd Weaselhead said, Maybe you should go to Alcoholics Anonymous.

The boys in their tassels and the girls in their pearls snickered, but Lai Fun didn't care because Lloyd Weaselhead talked to her. Talked to *her*. In *public*.

She loved Lloyd Weaselhead before and after she figured

out his crush on Corby Knudsen. No, she loved him *because* she knew. Knew that he was just like *her*. Except he was popular and she was a big fucking dweeb with her two dweeby friends and dweeby problems. They had once agreed to be twins separated at birth. She said, I'm gay too, Lloyd, and he said through his odd, boy-tears, Really? I think I am too, and she knew he was her *friend*.

Lloyd Weaselhead who's been married to the same woman for nearly twenty years. The goo of the past is already splattering her and she's only on the first page of the phonebook, well, the last page, working backwards.

Have you called Lloyd Weaselhead yet? asks Stefanja and Lai Fun says, Yes, but he must have call-waiting or something, there was no answering machine.

How far along are you with your names?

Far enough, thinks Lai Fun, because who has the time to waste a whole weekend walking in circles in a kitchen with a squirming toddler on one hip who's covered in jam and cat hair, and a telephone jammed between her head and shoulder? Who has the time to read the goddamn *phonebook*, or doodle with computer search engines on a keyboard full of cookie crumbs, and the cat digging in her bum with her tongue in front of the computer monitor while Lai Fun's little son plays trains up and down her legs? She pats Freddy's head every so often like he's a dog, to let her know she loves him – the experts say touch is an important medium for parent-child connection.

At this stage, Stefanja and Lai Fun are asking for addresses, a recent photo, and for people to fill out a cute questionnaire to go into a book for everyone to take home. (Where will you be in ten years? Where did you think you'd be now when you were eighteen?)

Conversations go like this:

Hello, can I speak to Margo Thesen?

May I ask who's calling?

Lai Fun Kugelheim. We went to high school together.

And then Margo Thesen, or Cathy Stilwell, or Rohan Bhagauti will get on the phone even though they are obviously in the tub or in the middle of sex or a fight at the kitchen sink and say, Oh my god, it's so great you called, what's your name again? Of course I'll give you my address, do you have a pen and paper. It's been years. I was wondering if a reunion was ever going to happen. (As if reunions pop up like pimples before a period, like gophers smushed in the road, like gusty chinook winds.)

Or sometimes they go:

I'm afraid I'll be travelling in Switzerland or having my ninth baby or cleaning out my ears with Q-Tips, but thank you for doing this, like they have mistaken her for a hooker with a heart of gold doing a favour for their homosexual son.

Surprisingly often, conversations go:

Hello, can I speak to Carol Zindel? Can I speak to Anne Winters? Michael Paperny?

A startled pause.

I'm sorry, Carol passed away three years ago, Anne died almost twenty years ago, Michael Paperny passed away last year ("passed away" is the popular phrase for recent deaths, for this year or two months ago), which makes Lai Fun stare hard at the yearbook photo of the person smiling or scowling or bored shitless or petrified in their gown and with a bouquet of roses, or in their dad's tie or both ("died" for five years or longer). She wonders, like Stefanja did with Kim, how come she never knew about it, wonders if she should have *known*. She remembers a whole flock of football players and gifted kids keeling over from cocaine heart attacks in Grade Eleven, she remembers Ramjit who died in a horse accident in Grade Ten, Kevin who stepped into an empty elevator shaft in Grade Twelve, but that covers only about eight people. Lai Fun doesn't know what to do with these new names at first when it becomes migraine-clear that there are more than one or two or seven. Crossing them out is unfair, too final. Putting an x by the name in the yearbook would be like they've done something wrong, and this is simply not the case. Maybe she should put a gold star, like when they scored perfectly on their spelling tests in Mrs Blake's Language Arts class. She puts a little crucifix beside the Christian ones, the ones with Ukrainian or Italian or Irish names, a little Star of David beside the ones she thinks maybe were Jewish, a little flower beside the Muslims, a tiny elephant beside the Hindus, an igloo beside the Jehovah's Witnesses because she is running out of ideas. A bat beside the ones who seem like they might have been atheists or agnostics or ended up in Hell.

Worse than the deaths are the:

You must have the wrong number, or;

There's no one here by that name, or;

Who?! or;

Click.

Or the ones where the phone just rings and rings and rings – no answering machine, no roommate, no kids, no mother, no nothing. They're just being assholes and ignoring the phone. Are they just too poor or too cheap or too lazy to get an answering machine or voice mail? She'll never know because they never answer their phones.

What the hell are you doing? says Angélique, who sneaked up the basement stairs to steal some matches. You're talking to yourself. You're talking really *loudly*.

Angélique stands in the doorway leading down to the basement. Freddy crawls to her and climbs up her long, black skirt.

Meow Freddy meow meow, says Angélique as she gently scratches his head and his cheeks and his bum with her nails like he is a kitten. Lai Fun can almost see teeth between Angélique's dark-red, lipsticked lips; teeth showing can mean Angélique's smiling – it would be a smile if Angélique ever truly smiled. Even when she laughs, her mouth looks more like a

71

trouser back-pocket than an eating, smiling, vomiting kind of mouth. So how come Freddy really loves her? He crawls like a marathon runner to Angélique. He only ever crawls away from Lai Fun.

Getting my reunion together, says Lai Fun. Getting my shit together.

Uh-umph! Angélique hoists Freddy up into her arms. Looks like you're doodling.

Those are the dead ones.

Angélique lifts Frederick above her head and barks into his face.

Ssssssss, says Freddy.

Did you hear me? Look at all these. Dead! They're all dead! It's an epidemic. We'd *better* have the reunion soon because there won't be any left if we wait.

Want me to take Frederick the Great for a walk? We can go to the café. Get Auntie a big fat soy café au lait.

Lai Fun mumbles into the phone book, Pissed away Saturday.

Stefanja rings the doorbell just as Angélique is leaving with Freddy cat-crawling each of his steps beside her as he pushes his own stroller, her cat's eye sunglasses on her nose and her lips dark red like she is some kind of Jacqueline Kennedy Onassis going incognito. The glamorous, tragic, spinster, older sister.

He needs a sweater! calls Lai Fun. She runs inside, then out to Freddy and Angélique. She throws a baby cardigan to Angélique, reaches out her arms to Freddy, puts her hands on both sides of his head and kisses his hair.

Stefanja looks after Angélique as she steps into the house.

Your sister never smiles, Stefanja says, and starts to cry. Her eyes red and shrunken because five of her names so far are dead and they hug each other tight, so tight. Lai Fun doesn't mention that six of hers died too – she doesn't want to steal the spotlight – or that two more passed away.

See? says Stefanja, wringing her hands like she is in a soap opera. This is what apathy leads to. Theresa, Pavitra, David B., Raj, Dennis, David C., all dead and did anyone bother to tell me? No. Could I go to the funerals and say goodbye? No. Look at this in my yearbook. It's from Dennis Chong. Listen: "Stephanie, I'm going to miss your never-ending smile and laughter. Good luck in everything you do and be happy. Dennis Chong."

This is the sweetest fucking thing I've ever read and now he's dead. Listen to this one from Theresa, "Your friend forever, Love, Theresa Agnew." I barely remember her, but she wrote this really nice message and now I can't ever say thank you. Did you ever get a hold of Lloyd? I'll try to call him. At least we know *he's* alive. Oh yes, and fucking Thor is having an *affair*!

Lai Fun hugs Stefanja tighter, Stefanja's tiny tiny bones, so Lai Fun doesn't have to look into her red-rimmed eyes.

How do you know?

You know how you know, you just know.

Stefanja's tears splatter the floor, the fridge. She wedges her sleeve under her weeping nose.

You know he knows you know, but is either of us going to tell the other we know? And here he is supposedly *writing*, working on his so-called *novel*, working on his brilliant *screen-play*, and his stupid wife makes sure the mortgage and the bills get paid, cleans up after him and his daughter.

Stefanja is making angry Xs in the dust on the microwave.

Are you going to say something? Lai Fun folds and unfolds a dishcloth, puts the dishcloth on top of her head, tucks the dishcloth under her elbow.

What's to say? We've been married so long. I don't want Olivia to have to zigzag between two parents. He's a big, forty-year-old baby, but he's the man I married and the man I love and the father of my child and my big yellow bear. We will get through this. I will sign us up for marriage counselling right now. A big, yellow teddy bear of a man, he is. *My* teddy bear.

A gold strand of Stefanja's hair falls in her face. She sucks up the snot and wipes her eyes with the palms of her hands.

I feel a little bit sorry for the stupid twat he's fucking, that's what. Dork doesn't know how much we love each other. She is up against a mighty force of nature, home-wrecking evil lady.

Maybe the evil lady's an evil gentleman, says Lai Fun.

Yeah! Maybe she's a he! I doubt it. Thor is a big homophobe.

Yeah. That's a little harsh, but I understand what you mean.

Harsh? I should wring her ears off. Oof! breathes Stefanja. I feel so much better now after having talked to you. Everything's going to be fine. Everything! I can feel it. You're so right. Thor and I will make marriage counselling *a blast*!

Lai Fun will stop meeting Thor for sex. Never again. Never. It's the pregnancy hormones, she will fight the hormones. She will turn over a new leaf. She feels her branches already shaking. She will not be a twat. She rubs her ear.

My ears hurt. I'm tired of phoning, she says.

I'll phone Lloyd, says Stefanja. Lloyd'll know what to do.

CHAPTER 6

Even though it is the end of May, Sunday night it snows so hard buses slide diagonally down the Centre Street bridge. Lai Fun puts on her parka, boots, toque, and mittens; she straps Freddy to her back, and trudges into the cold of the snowstorm.

Baby-gear bag hooked over her shoulder and tucked just under her armpit. Baby strapped to her back, Freddy idly catching snow flakes in his mittens, he licks at the invisible cold. Great chunks of snow drop around them, and Lai Fun steps carefully over the black puddles as she crosses intersections. Because it's always winter in this city, winter is one long snowstorm broken by the occasional delirious chinook. Delirious was the last time Lai Fun made love to Jennifer (so long ago she can barely remember), Jennifer deliberately bouncing the bed. That last time she felt like Jennifer might actually mind if Lai Fun wasn't around.

She puts a big X through Thor.

An old man saunters on ahead of Lai Fun. He wears an old-fashioned cape that whips around his legs, he wears a beret, he wears leather gloves. Certain old men make her nervous, but men in capes are superheroes. Lai Fun walks faster. The old man hums words from an old French song from when she was a child in French immersion school:

et la mer efface sur le sable
les pas des amants désunis

October next year they will blow up her old school. Who will blow up the school, Lai Fun is not so sure, but it will blow, just like the hospital where her mother worked was blown up, just like she could blow, so will the old sandstone school blow, doesn't matter how many lives passed through it, doesn't matter if it was built before the Vikings. She should forget the reunion; she should just let the class of '85 go straight to hell like the self-involved pack of losers it's been for twenty years. On the other hand, they were *her* pack, even if she never felt a part of them. They're tied by landscape, by geography. The thought of seeing Hadley Constable with permanent bags under her eyes and a middle-aged woman's belly makes it all seem worthwhile. Aging teenagers like to be invited to reunions, believe themselves pursued like rare sex objects.

The old man turns the corner ahead of her and his cape whips around like he is some kind of Dracula, like he is some kind of Pierre Elliott Trudeau, and he walks into the Rose Café. Lai Fun tries the door – she has run out of coffee – but the door is locked. The café is closed and she has been tricked by the snow into seeing French-Canadian superheroes. She peers inside the front window. Sees the silhouette of a stone griffin screaming at her from behind the cappuccino machine. Last night she dreamed of the welcome mat by the back door.

The whirling snow shouts a long list of names at Lai Fun. Names she has no hope of finding, flipping through the phone book, the yearbook: names that have changed, names moved to other continents, names who've died, or names that have disappeared. And what about people who dropped out before graduating or moved to a different school? Are they invited? If she can remember and can locate them in two phone calls or less. Otherwise they bloody well lose out. Her ear hurts in the wind.

Lai Fun and Freddy walk through the snow in the approaching night, the sky above them the colour of coat hangers. As Lai Fun and Freddy make their way back towards the house, the street lamps behind them light up one by one by one.

CHAPTER 7

Cocktails, dinner, a dance. The next day brunch, then a softball game in the afternoon. Each event will have a title. So far the first event is called "Wow Have You Changed!," the last night will be called "Had Enough Yet?" Other possibilities are "You Sure Clean Up Good" for the formal dinner, and a "Where'd All My Hair Go?" event. A banner with "Stay Proud, Stay True, Stay Real" at every event. The softball day is up for discussion – either "Too Feeble for Fastball" or "Trojans Forever." Lai Fun wants bowling because she'll be too pregnant and exhausted to do anything but chuck balls at pins and she figures everyone will be out of shape anyway, but Hadley Constable and Lloyd Weaselhead – ex-captain of the Trojans football team, the fastball team, the basketball team, the uncloseted closeted gay singing sunshine – want softball and what Hadley Constable and Lloyd Weaselhead want, they get. Back then. Back now.

Lai Fun and Stefanja are trapped in Hadley Constable's living room with Hadley and Lloyd: Hadley's chair is in front of the doorway leading out of the house. Lai Fun looks at Stefanja sideways. Stefanja is too busy bubbling and purring to Hadley about Hadley's beautiful house, lovely floors, charming walls, exquisite garbage can to notice Lai Fun. Lai Fun stuffs a broccoli spear into her mouth.

What Stefanja and Lai Fun planned as a modest, single night get-together has, in Lloyd and Hadley's grabby hands, become a four-day extravaganza. Softball instead of bowling, one night at a sports bar for drinks and pool and an informal buffet dinner, next morning a brunch with children, then all-day football, lunch at a seafood restaurant owned by Lloyd and Maureen Weaselhead, née Jones, who married Lloyd Weaselhead right after high school, followed by a massive pool party and barbeque to which Lai Fun is almost 100 percent sure she won't be invited and no doubt bad booze-breath and husband-swapping and more football stories and a lot of hair ruined from chlorine. Whoever heard of swimming right after lunch?

Stefanja was part of Hadley's crowd because she was obvious Hadley material – she wore the trendy pants that inspired Kim Shisamoto to name them the Baked Potato People: those 1980s, expensive, pleated puffy pants that tapered down around the ankles so the five girls' asses looked like baked potatoes. Supposed to look so *sexy* because they're rich-rich-Richie Rich – just like the other rich kids in their alligator Lacoste shirts and Polo sweaters and Drakkar men's cologne who got to drive their parents' BMWs and Volvos. Stefanja was invited to all the Lloyd Weaselhead-hosted football parties at Hadley's house. Stefanja was also pretty enough and her family well-off enough to be a Baked Potato Person, but then one night Stefanja slept with another Potato's Trojan – or maybe the Trojan just leered at her in front of a field-hockey witness, maybe Stefanja said the wrong thing in an Eastern European language – because tout de suite sans warning Stefanja was banished to the realm of the Shit People where Lai Fun and Kim resided.

There's no way Lai Fun would have been included as a Baked Potato, ever, no way at all. Too keen. Too spastic. Too poor after her dad lost his job.

Lai Fun had a hysterical crush on Lloyd (everyone did, it was the way, no one could resist Lloyd) until she fell all over his secret. After that, she adored him. His picture in the yearbook, the heavy football shoulders, the tight, eighteen-year-old thighs. Lloyd Weaselhead whom she caught necking with Corby Knudsen in the drama room. Who didn't kill her when she told him she saw, but instead became her secret best friend. And she, the nerd! He was the secret ally of Lai Fun, 100 percent nerd certified! How she adored Lloyd Weaselhead and their secret pact. True friends forever. Lai Fun glowers at Stefanja, Lloyd, and Hadley – what's Stefanja doing? – and wants to chop off all their heads and bowl them down the stairs.

Stefanja's mistake is that she won't tell Hadley Constable to butt out – it's Stefanja and Lai Fun's show. She asked Hadley to help organize the door prizes with them and then Hadley Constable, who's the president of the Alumni Association, and Lloyd Weaselhead, a TV sports anchor with his own prairie seafood restaurant chain, decided they needed a four-hour meeting to discuss the reunion.

Well, says Hadley Constable brightly in her taupe and eggshell living room with maroon accents. So what have you all been doing for the past, oh, twenty years?

Hadley, Stefanja, Maureen who wasn't even invited, and Lloyd laugh contentedly.

Lai Fun could hurl in her chair, the baby a pressing bruise under her ribs. She takes a quick sip of water.

Lai Fun, you're pregnant! says Hadley, her eyes shift to Lai Fun's ring finger. Congratulations. What does your husband do?

Lai Fun bites down, ferocious, on the neck of her water bottle. Lloyd coughs into his hand. Her hackles shoot up, her pupils dilate, she's just about to leap in for a chunk of Hadley's throat when Stefanja says, Lai Fun's partner Jennifer works at Gargoyle Communications. Jennifer's the Communications Supervisor, right, Lai Fun? She's very high up in the company.

Lai Fun looks at Stefanja and her eyes start to fill. She is fucking Stefanja's husband and Stefanja is her best friend.

Of course! says Hadley. Well, congratulations on the baby, Lai Fun. Wendell and I are trying too. Still have a few years left!

It's so *nice* to see everyone, burbles Stefanja. So *homey*. Like I've come home again!

We need to do this reunion right, so let's get started, says Lloyd Weaselhead, like he is some sort of motivational speaker with pancake makeup on his extra-wide jaws. His ring finger has a giant wedding band and Maureen beams at his right side. This is not the Lloyd Lai Fun loved. This is the Lloyd she met in the halls virtually every morning. Every afternoon. Who pretended he didn't know her, because their pact was a *secret* pact.

It was Lloyd's idea to have a formal meeting; Hadley's idea to have the meeting at her house, show off her teak furniture, her Barcelona mosaics. It was Hadley's husband Wendell's idea – not invited, either – to strike ad hoc committees, and it was Lai Fun's idea that they should all bring their lunches because she was pregnant and needed to keep her sugar levels up and she didn't trust Hadley not to go cheap on snacks.

We need to write up a mandate, says Hadley.

We don't need a mandate! For god's sake! says Lai Fun, shoving on the fetus's head – fetus does a double-flip and offers Lai Fun the heel of its foot.

Our mandate is to have a goddamn reunion!

She bites into an apple and the apple sprays the room.

If you don't want to be part of the mandate committee, Lai Fun, says Lloyd Weaselhead, you just have to say so. He turns his back to Lai Fun. What we need to do, Hadley, Lloyd says, showing his grim sports anchor smile, is strategic planning.

Should we hire a consultant? asks Hadley, patting her $89 pillows from Chintz & Company. Taupe *and* maroon. We'll have to find room for it in the budget. Maureen, do you want to make a motion?

Lai Fun wants to make a motion with her middle finger, she can barely stop herself. She studies Hadley's mouth, her lips and teeth barking out mandates and strategic plans and softball schedules, and wonders if Hadley keeps tabs on Wendell with mandates and strategic plans.

I don't think we need to make a motion, says Maureen, smiling up at Lloyd.

Let's do it anyway, says Lloyd. I move that the '85 Reunion Organizers look into – no – investigate the possibility of hiring a consultant for the purpose of strategic planning.

We need a seconder. Lai Fun?

Lai Fun twists on the couch, she twists her wedding band around and around on her finger. She picks at two new zits she's sprouted. One on each side of her forehead, just like horns.

Seconded by Lai Fun. Now, all in favour? asks Hadley. Next item of business: Hiring a caterer.

My restaurant, says Lloyd.

Perfect, says Hadley. Maureen beams some more. Stefanja, says Hadley, you and Maureen prepare three possible dinner menus and submit them to us for consideration by a week from today.

Lai Fun closes her eyes. When they open, she is staring at Lloyd, Lloyd the betrayer, and remembers the hug and kiss on the cheek Lloyd gave her, his tears – she was sure – on her cheek. She remembers the scratch of his stubble; he doesn't bloody remember, that much is clear. Lai Fun keeps her mouth shut. He looks better than he did when he was eighteen and much better in person than on TV with all that make-up and plastic hair. All the puppy fat gone and his face tighter with crow's feet around the eyes and lines around his mouth from laughing at two decades of guests' banal sports jokes.

Lai Fun turns from Lloyd and stares at Hadley Constable, whose eyeliner is painted in straight, perfect lines around her eyes, but her eyelashes are caked with mascara, foundation flattening the scars of zit bumps on her jaw. Hadley's crow's feet have marched their way around her eyes, around her mouth, and left behind jowls. No grey hairs to speak of, only more wrinkles, softer skin between the wrinkles, a hint of a belly tucked in the belt of her linen suit, diamond stud earrings. Lai Fun fingers her own earringless ears because if she had earrings her ears would be bloody scraps from Freddy yanking them out. Even if she were wearing earrings, she would never go so obvious as diamonds the size of cherry pits. She left the diamond earrings Jennifer gave her for their fifth anniversary at home. Hadley has taken the afternoon off from her father's law firm.

So this is what's going to happen, says Lloyd, and Lai Fun remembers that he always was an arrogant fuck, even when he was six years old in Grade One with only three hairs on his entire head and his incredibly bony fists the only thing going for him, and then he lays out his and Hadley's hijacking plans for the entire reunion and Lai Fun wants to spear out his eyeballs with her mechanical pencil.

Lloyd Weaselhead and Hadley Constable have planned everything, it turns out, no need for consensus here: booking the sports bar – the one where the hospital used to be because it's right next to Lloyd's newest prairie seafood restaurant – the cocktail bar, the pool, the school baseball field, the decorations, the mini-yearbook.

The sports bar where the General Hospital used to be? asks Stefanja.

Have you been inside it? asks Lai Fun.

Lloyd smiles at her with his mouth but not his eyes and Lai Fun feels her heart go soggy like a rotten peach at the bottom of the fruit bowl. Especially when she remembers him wearing that pearl necklace to the Hallowe'en dance, Grade Twelve, and all the girls going into heat – presenting their rumps to him – especially Maureen Jones swanning around his locker and hanging off the chain link fence in the teacher's parking lot, watching

Lloyd during football practice while all the while Lai Fun *knew*.

Lai Fun knew all about Lloyd. She sees him now, behind the Japanese garden *Mikado* set in the empty school auditorium, eating up Corby Knudsen's mouth with his own, Corby pushed up against the wall and Lloyd all over Corby's mouth with his lips and tongue and breath, licking Corby's chest in the V of his Lacoste shirt. That same night Lloyd giving Lai Fun a giant, spontaneous hug because she's told him she likes girls just the same way he likes Corby. Lloyd Weaselhead. Traitor! That was October 31.

By January 9, Lloyd had his hands all over Maureen. Lloyd a victim of peer-pressure Baked Potato People blackmail, the heterosexual hysteria that made Lai Fun thrill with a Godzilla-sized crush when Lloyd Weaselhead hugged her and kissed her cheek and ensured that she had in fact been kissed by a boy, kissed by the most popular boy in the school even though the kiss was not romantic, it was not about *boys and girls* or *birds and bees*. The terrible need to belong.

CHAPTER 8

Lai Fun is tired of all the snow. Just snow and snow and more snow. No sun, she longs for sun, it's almost a full day since she's seen the sun and it's already affecting her brain. Hadley and Lloyd are just the beginning of that high school horror. She will have to see them all at once and is she ready to see them all? Of course not and for sure. She hates the vortex of the computer, looking for email addresses, websites, footprints. She hates her ear crunching against the telephone receiver, hates scribbling addresses onto envelopes that get returned in three days flat. The only reason she isn't jettisoning the whole project is because Maureen and Hadley and Lloyd said she could be in charge of "Wow Have You Changed." She will kick their asses, it will be so good. And Stefanja would hate Lai Fun forever if Lai Fun bailed. And Lai Fun owes Stefanja, she knows she owes her.

Lai Fun pulls on her toque, snaps off Freddy's television show, and hooks her bag around her shoulder. Freddy screams, his hands stretched toward the empty television screen. Lai Fun clumps through the snow up the hill from her house, Freddy bundled and screaming on her back in his layers of fleece and baby-sized Gore-Tex and rabbit-ear hat and crocheted blanket because she made him leave his *Run Rabbit Run* show before it was done. She smashes through snow all the way to the dog park, the one with the hill, the one where she can see the giant snowing sky, pink and brown and green reflected in the bubbling clouds, a violent glass of iced tea above her head as the west wind rears up, gusts above and blusters around them. Freddy screams into the open mouth of the arriving chinook wind. And Lai Fun starts to scream too. She screams into the snowy, relentless, windswept sky. She screams a duet with Freddy – the wind swoops and swirls and pitches her voice so everyone will hear her: ANSWER YOUR PHONES, YOU ASSHOLES!

Louve and Fritz-Peter jolt awake from their sleeps – they both have to work tonight. Louve reaches for the phone, but Lai Fun isn't on the other end. Stefanja jumps off the tread-mill, suddenly sick to her stomach, Thor mumbles about crane-shots, Olivia grabs her bunny's ear harder. Maureen Weasel-head has just finished maneuvering with both hands to make Lloyd Weaselhead come and she dozes under a patina of sweat, while Lloyd suddenly opens his eyes to the blank ceiling. Hadley looks for her lost diamond earring under the bed and finds another one, made of moulded plastic. Somewhere, a griffin yawns and blinks.

THERE'S A FUCKING REUNION! Lai Fun shouts, loud enough to wake the dead.

PART II

THE WAY OF ELEMENTARY SCHOOL

CHAPTER 9

Louve sends Lai Fun off to the best school possible, French school, in this prairie town where Louve and Fritz-Peter smell manure instead of flowers and the trees slide from green to brown to skeleton then back to green because there is no spring or autumn here. Not like back home in Ottawa. Maybe this is why Lai Fun becomes a homosexual. Because there are no natural changes of the seasons around her as a baby. A French school because the Canada they want, the daughter they want, is special and bilingual, because they do not want Lai Fun to become one of *them*, the status quo. Louve can't even buy groceries without being harassed by some hick.

Are you from Montréal? shouts a man, he carries a grocery bag in one arm and a camera in the other hand. She smashes the camera out of his hand with her open palm.

I'm from Ottawa! she shouts back at his boring shoes. She jumps off the curb and runs across the street in her leather micro miniskirt and flashing legs.

Aren't many people look like you, shouts the man. Just wanted to take a picture to show the wife!

The fact that Fritz-Peter is from Ottawa is not as noticeable until he opens his mouth, parts his lips in his sharp little goatee.

I am from Ottawa, he snarls in his accent. I am Canadian.

Lai Fun is smarter than Mozart, than Einstein, than Marie Curie. October, and it should be autumn, but Louve can smell snow on the horizon. Louve has brushed Lai Fun's hair into three pigtails fastened with those ball hair-fasteners that look like bubble gum because this is what Lai Fun wants.

Then Louve haphazardly smoothes her own hair and tucks it up with too many bobby-pins that spring from her head as she walks Lai Fun across the street to the school bus stop. She knows the neighbours are watching her from behind their blinds, their curtains, through frosted brown glass. Watching the only black lady on the street and her half black, half white little daughter walk across the avenue like their walking is the Second Coming. Her neighbours' lives must be troglodytically boring.

Stand on the other side of the street, Mama, Lai Fun says.

I can do this by myself, she says.

Lai Fun such a big girl and Louve watches her small daughter who has just disowned her disappear inside the school bus, not even waving goodbye.

Louve looks down at her chest and walks. She doesn't like the way her white nurse's uniform gathers around the middle of her rib-cage and makes her breasts droop like a dog's teats, but this is the only ironed uniform she has in the house and there is no time to iron another one. She knows Maybelline and Robert, the white, retired, Scottish couple in 1102, are watching her. She and Fritz-Peter and Lai Fun are always being watched. Like they are exotic animals or friendly monsters, Maybelline asking to touch Lai Fun's hair and Louve sweeping Lai Fun away from Maybelline's tentacle fingers and into the house without another word. Maybelline and Robert, the window blink-blink of albino gophers peeping from their holes.

In the hospital cafeteria, to keep herself from thinking about Lai Fun's five-year-old betrayal, Louve and Dr Stoker – the only doctor who'll talk to the nurses like they're human – discuss Margaret Trudeau's breakdown. Their own unofficial lunch-time book club. In the time before book clubs. In the time when there was such a thing as lunch-times because the major hospital staff cutbacks and implosions hadn't happened yet and when you could smoke without having to go and smoke with the corpses.

She's a flower-child, says Dr Stoker, and Louve thinks of Lai Fun. They have weak constitutions, those flower-children, he says.

Louve unwraps her sandwich carefully. Bread with alfalfa sprouts. A Styrofoam cup of coffee with the edges chewed up in scalloped patterns by her own pointy teeth. She lights a cigarette.

Poor thing, says Louve. Pierre Trudeau works too much and leaves her alone too much.

In other news, this may sound petty, says Dr Stoker, but what makes Margaret Trudeau think she has taste? Dr Stoker taps his cigarette on the edge of the ashtray. I don't understand it. I come from Vancouver too and the god of taste did not suddenly descend upon *me* out of the Okanagan interior. Or was I waiting at the wrong bus stop? They say the walls at 24 Sussex are wallpapered with *silk*.

Silk wallpaper! Fritz-Peter and I are looking at wallpaper, we even saw grass wallpaper, but not once was I presented with the option of *silk* wallpaper. Just because you have money doesn't mean you're suddenly blessed with taste.

She's too young for him. He's thirty years older, for crying out loud. It's too *old*!

Age isn't the problem, says Louve. It's their different backgrounds. She's a flower-child as you've said. He neglects her.

She clicks and unclicks the fastener of her cigarette case. Obviously Stoker's forgotten Louve is older than Fritz-Peter.

Well, I *like* her, Dr Stoker suddenly pronounces.

Me too. She'll figure it out.

Louve looks at the clock high up on the cafeteria wall, the seconds and milliseconds ticking away. Time to get back to work, she says. The show must go on. Catheters must be inserted, silk wallpaper or no silk wallpaper.

Louve crushes her fifth cigarette into the ashtray.

Telephone for you, Louve! calls another nurse.

And Louve rushes away from the book-and-cigarette club, takes the phone and listens for a moment to the voice on the other end of the phone and says, Well, is she all right? She's not sick? This number is only for emergencies!

Louve props the phone between her shoulder and ear, looks at the stack of charts on the desk, fiddles in her pocket with a wad of gauze stiff with dried blood. One of her bells is going off.

I have to get back to work now, says Louve. Please don't call me again unless it's an emergency. Call her father next time. I can't come running to the phone for every little thing.

Betrayer. Betrayed.

And Louve hangs up. Smells her fingers. Tries to scrape at least some of the blood out from under her thumbnails. Runs after her bell.

The last time Louve had to talk to someone at the school was in September when Lai Fun told Louve that the art teacher was murdered and all the children were forced to attend the funeral. Lai Fun came back with a story of looking at the dead body of Mr Smiley in his coffin, an axe protruding from the head, his skin pale and wrinkled, and Louve phoned the school and while she waited to speak to the principal, she lit another cigarette, and drilled the heel of her hand into her forehead.

Mr Smiley the art teacher has passed away for undisclosed reasons, Mrs Kugelheim, says the principal. But none of the children were taken to the funeral. I don't know where Lai Fun could have gotten that idea.

Since giving birth to Lai Fun, sometimes Louve is so tired that when she gets into bed at night, she looks forward to the nap she'll have tomorrow.

Louve and Fritz-Peter's Lai Fun is their Love Child, their glorious Canadian proclamation, and more gifted than Picasso although not as big a pig. She was made the night Pierre Elliott Trudeau – with his crooked, sexy smile – announced that the state had no business in the bedrooms of the nation. Louve said, I'm too old for another baby! but Pierre Elliott and Fritz-Peter seduced her into a long, luxurious session of tremendous, patriotic love-making. And even though Lai Fun was born in western Canada, she will be a child of all of Canada, of leaf-bright autumns and spring coastal rains and Great Lake boating and Newfoundland ice storms. Maybelline and Robert or no Maybelline and Robert. Trudeau and his new immigration policy have made sure everyone is welcome in this country. *Everyone.*

Those teachers at Lai Fun's school, especially Mrs Hilda Blake, will have to understand the magic that is Lai Fun – their wonderful, bicultural, bilingual baby who suddenly at the age of six has no heart – and that Lai Fun's father can answer the phone just as easily at his job as Louve can at hers.

What is that? Give me that, Lou-Anne! commands Mrs Blake, but Lai Fun, being the much younger second daughter of Louve and Fritz-Peter and a child of Trudeau's mania and sexual liberation, slips the candy into her mouth and swallows it whole which almost chokes her. She looks down at Mrs Blake's feet, so long, the beige, rubber-soled shoes.

My name is Lai Fun, Lai Fun coughs out. Not Lou-Anne!
What's your Canadian name, then? asks Mrs Blake.
I don't –
Mrs Blake grabs Lai Fun's jaws and pries them open. She

sweeps out Lai Fun's mouth with her index finger. Mrs Blake wipes her finger off with a Kleenex from her cardigan sleeve.

Your finger tastes like dog! shouts Lai Fun.

What an infraction!

Eating during recess. Eating only happens during lunch, during heavily supervised, regimented lunch, *not* recess. Candy shaped like a fingertip. With a nail on it. Looked like a real fingertip. Whatever it was, the child swallowed it whole, the child swallowed it during recess instead of lunch. Dirty Lou-Anne, a little black girl with a Chinese name. Badly brought up Lou-Anne, disgusting enough to pick up any old thing, a fallen fingernail, a piece of doll, and pop it in her mouth. Except that none of the other children near Lou-Anne hold dolls with missing limbs.

I am going to send you to the principal. Remove your hat! No hats indoors! snaps Mrs Blake, and as she swipes the toque off Lai Fun's head, Lai Fun begins to whine like a puppy which reassures Mrs Blake that Mrs Blake hasn't entirely lost the battle. Especially since there's no way she would ever send a child like Lou-Anne to the principal, Monsieur Agapsowich. The most effeminate, ineffectual heterosexual man Mrs Blake has ever seen. Mrs Blake can work her own spells.

I need my hat, sobs Lai Fun. I'll get in trouble if I lose it.

I'm phoning your mother, Lou-Anne Kugelheim. I will keep your hat with me until after school. You will stop crying *now*, orders Mrs Blake, or I really will send you to the principal's office. Don't let me see that thumb of yours go anywhere *near* your mouth. Or your nose!

Mrs Blake shoos away the other kids, Stefanja, Kim, Lloyd Weaselhead, and bends down to Lai Fun's ear: Lou-Anne, she whispers, You're ordinary. You're *not* more special than any of the other children.

Lai Fun stops crying and stares.

I am remarkable, chokes out Lai Fun. I'm smarter than Mozart, than Einstein, than Marie Curie.

Mrs Blake in her giant, rubber-soled shoes strides away with Lai Fun's hat.

That afternoon Mrs Blake tells her to stop making such a racket with her desk-drawer and that the class has heard from Miss Smarty-Pants Lou-Anne already today, let other people have a chance to speak!

Probably the new teacher, Mlle Tremblay, was wearing false nails and that's what the child popped into her mouth. Mrs Blake is entirely sure Mlle Tremblay wears fake eyelashes, her eyes inappropriately big and brown and wet. Mlle Tremblay who belly-danced at the last school assembly with a scimitar balanced on her head and all the teachers and pupils and Monsieur Agapsowich clapping madly to the music. This never would have happened in the old days with the old principal before French started being taught in schools and shoved down honest, Canadian throats. Schools going to pot. Mlle Tremblay, on the playground now, walking among the scrambling and screaming children with her hands clasped behind her back, her brown hair swept into an elaborate chignon on the back of her head, pays no attention to the illegal eating on the playground, but Mlle Tremblay is a pushover who can barely speak English to boot.

Mrs Blake looks around for Miss Dranchuk, the Grade Four teacher, one of the normal ones. But Miss Dranchuk is laughing with Mlle Tremblay, the both of them on the other side of the schoolyard, surrounded by children pulling at their skirts. Seduced by the French menace. The French peril.

Hatred runs up the front of Mrs Blake's dress like a feral cat.

Eating at recess. Eating *junk food* at recess.

Mrs Blake phones Mrs Kugelheim to tell her about Lou-Anne insisting on wearing her hat indoors and report the swallowed piece of candy Lou-Anne stole from another child. That gets her nowhere. She phones Lou-Anne's father.

I crocheted that toque! says Fritz-Peter. Why shouldn't she wear it? Have you asked her why she needs to wear it?

She says it keeps her Einstein brain warm. (Men crocheting!)

Well, what's wrong with that? says Fritz-Peter. If her head is cold, then she has the good sense to wear a hat!

Mrs Hilda Blake drills the tip of her pencil into the table top.

Lou-Anne –

Who?

Lai – Mrs Blake grinds her jaws – *Fewwwn* is a distraction in class, Mr Kugelheim. Her attention wanders and her attachment to the hat is just a manifestation of this. She says she can't think without it. What utter nonsense. Perhaps she should be in a less demanding environment. Perhaps we should take her out of the French programme and put her in with the regulars.

She hears hyperventilating across the wires.

Look, Mrs Blake, says Fritz-Peter. Lai Fun reads to my wife every night before bedtime. She gets her way through every single sentence. Einstein was diagnosed as autistic as a child. Trudeau didn't get a real job until he was forty years old. People develop at different speeds. I have an idea: give her only French classes. She loves Mlle Tremblay. Ask Mlle Tremblay, she knows things. Does Lai Fun need to take English classes? Perhaps it bores her. Perhaps English classes are too slow for her.

Of course Lai Fun's father would think Mlle Tremblay a superior teacher with her long eyelashes and short skirts. Mrs Blake blinks furiously. Belly-dancing, crocheting men, and French. They will strangle her!

All the kids in Lai Fun's class know the Green group is the dumb kids in Reader Two and the Yellow group the smart kids in Reader Five. The Blue kids are in Reader Three, and the Red

Group in Reader Four. All the kids, including Lai Fun, know that the little group of five – the Orange Group – that leaves the class Thursday afternoons for the whole afternoon, is the super-dumb retardo kids who need extra help because they can't even figure out Reader Zero, can't tell time, can't tell the difference between nickels and dimes to save their lives. Paul. Lai Fun. Lloyd. Haroun. Kim. Daisy. Ozzie the Mennonite.

All the kids know whose families can afford Barbie camper sets, the Barbie sports car, the whole Barbie spread. Whose families can't or don't: the weird immigrants' kids, Kim and Lai Fun, with their fried fish and banana smell or raw fish in black boxes for lunch. Others who can't or won't are all the pasty white kids like Ozzie the Mennonite with their bowl-haircuts smelling of raw, dyed meat and sour milk and bread and succumbing to the school lice epidemics every time. For those kids, school is a fork jammed into the middle of the forehead.

But, except for Mrs Blake, Lai Fun *loves* school; school inspires her with a passion no falling knee socks or frizzy hair or shouts of "Paki!" or "Hey, Kung Fu!" or "Are you from Africa?" or classes for dumbos can hold back. She is excellent at aiming the ball in four-square and at a later age could make an excellent wedding co-ordinator, for she has the gift of multi-tasking. Mrs Blake calls it hyperactivity, but Fritz-Peter and Louve recognize her gift. Some would call Pierre Trudeau's world travels and beard-growing, his indoor pool and skiing vacations, his sliding down banisters and pretending to fall down stairs, his staring protesters down in the middle of flying bottles, his spontaneous dancing with beautiful women hyperactivity and easily distracted, no? Fritz-Peter and Louve would not be surprised if Lai Fun became Prime Minister of Canada. Their little angel. Their little coconut-headed seraph.

Lai Fun is in love with every French teacher – wraps her arms and legs around Mlle Tremblay, sings earnestly, lips rounding out the vowels and six-year-old teeth tapping out consonants to Monsieur Agapsowich's ukulele strumming, "Alouette, gentille Alouette!"; they pretend they are all Gilles Vigneault lilting "Mon pays, ce n'est pas un pays c'est l'hiver!" and her heart trills like it's at the beach when she sees Monsieur Agapsowich's leather sandal tapping along to the music, sandals just like her daddy's. And when she tells Monsieur Agapsowich or Mlle Tremblay about how she saw the griffins on the bridge fluttering and flapping their wings like her budgie Max does at home they smile and sing some more.

Mrs Blake, the English teacher, is another story. That Creamsicle of a woman with her blonde, perfect page-boy.

She holds up a large feather.

Indians wear feathers as part of their costumes, she says.

Lloyd, she calls, show the class how to wear this feather. Tell us what this feather means.

I don't know, says Lloyd, picking his nose and wiping the goobers on the underside of his desk.

Lloyd, tell us about this feather! Take your finger away from your nose!

I don't *know*, Lloyd says loud.

He blubbers, the feather dangling in his hand.

Mrs Blake blinks at Lloyd for a moment, then takes the feather in her hand.

They wear them like this! Mrs Blake says, and holds the feather at the back of her hair, page-boy sleek. The feather sticks straight up like a flag-pole.

In the schoolyard, kids come up to Lloyd and say "How, kemosabe!" then run away laughing until he swings out his fist and Mrs Blake in her rubber-soled shoes sneaks up behind him and sends him to Monsieur Agapsowich's office.

Mrs Blake makes Lai Fun stay in the Orange Group even though she can read all the way through Reader One, tries to steal the candy Fritz-Peter made especially for Lai Fun, grinds her knuckle into the tops of the heads of kids like Paul and

Ozzie, knocks her stapler on Lloyd's head, breaks her wooden pointer over Haroun's desk.

No, draw yourself with this one, says Mrs Blake. Black is the name of your skin and the black crayon is the one you should use to colour in the skin on your self-portrait, Lou-Anne. See, class? Isn't black a better colour for Lou-Anne?

Mrs Blake tries to make Lai Fun hate the silvery taste of her own saliva, the slick movement of her own eyeballs up and down, side to side in their sockets. Lai Fun the weirdo in her crayon-black skin.

One afternoon when it's raining too hard and they stay inside for recess, Mrs Blake leans down close to Lai Fun's ear as though about to whisper and then suddenly latches onto Lai Fun's neck with her teeth like she does with some of the other kids (except Lloyd who clocks her with his giant bony knuckles and gets sent to Monsieur Agapsowich's office for the strap), but Lai Fun lashes out with her fingers like a cat just like her parents taught her if attacked by a wacko and she neatly scrapes Mrs Blake's jaw and Lai Fun has to go to Monsieur Agapsowich's office too. She pees her pants in terror and shame because she likes Monsieur Agapsowich so much. Her bum and her pride soaking wet.

Lai Fun sits in her chair and waits for Louve or Fritz-Peter to come pick her up, she doesn't know which, she doesn't know how mad the one will be, and Monsieur Agapsowich looks at her from over his desk with such big, frowny eyes Lai Fun cries and cries, snot dripping down her lips and onto the yucky brown checkered pants the secretary found in the Lost and Found box. Her own wet pants in a plastic bread bag for taking home.

The bags under Louve's eyes even darker than usual when she sits down beside Lai Fun. Louve feels three hundred years old. She still wears her nurse's uniform. Three patients coded today, one right after the other. Two died. She would kill for a cigarette, but smoked the last one at the bus stop on the way down to the school and her mother-of-pearl cigarette case is empty. Fritz-Peter sits on the other side of Lai Fun. He picks up the bread bag with the pants inside it, sniffs it, and tucks the bag into the empty front section of his briefcase.

Mummy, Mrs Blake tried to bite me! says Lai Fun.

Nonsense. What utter nonsense, says Mrs Blake. She sits with her arms crossed in a chair to the left of Agapsowich's desk.

I did this! Lai Fun says, and Lai Fun cuts at the air with her fingers in imitation of herself. Louve's face takes on a very concentrated look at Mrs Blake. Louve looks like when she is straightening her hair in the mirror using the hot comb and knows danger is near.

First you tell the children about a teacher's unsolved death without consulting the parents, then I get confronted with this! You tried to *bite* her? My daughter is here to learn French, not how to fight like an animal. Obviously you provoked her, Mrs Blake.

Now, now, says Monsieur Agapsowich, smiling at the two women as if he hears ukulele strains. I know this is unusual behaviour. Lai Fun is usually a good girl. Would you like a glass of mineral water?

Always a good girl, says Fritz-Peter. I would like a glass, yes.

I would like to know what teaching credentials Mrs Blake has, Monsieur Agapsowich, says Louve. Has she never worked with little children before? Lai Fun tells me ridiculous, violent stories about funerals and biting teachers. She's not living a fairy tale.

I have been teaching at this school since before the school board opened it, says Mrs Blake. Are you outlawing fairy tales?

Then why is my daughter peeing her pants twice a week? Mrs Blake, don't you know what Lai Fun is? She is *very* sensitive.

She is as smart as Trudeau, as Marie Curie. Stories you tell her come to life in her head. She is so creative she hears animals and constellations *talk*. She has the soul of an artist. She believes that you, Mrs Blake, suck the blood of her classmates. She screams in the night because she says you suck blood from her friends who are *living human beings*.

Mrs Blake wrinkles her nose at Louve. What am I, asks Mrs Blake, a walking metaphor? A child pees her pants. Blame the teacher. A child gets a nightmare. Blame the teacher.

Monsieur Agapsowich taps a sandalled foot.

The stories you tell them are simply too frightening, says Louve, snapping the latch of her cigarette case up and down.

Fritz-Peter tries his charm on Mrs Blake, he looks more like the people in this town, his skin is pink and white, not a dark brown like Louve's; he smiles and purrs: Lai Fun is not like other children. She needs consideration, and sometimes this means just a bit more patience. Surely you know what I mean, Mrs Blake. No more unsolved deaths. No more bad stories. No more provoking her.

Let me reassure you, Mr Kugelhcim, says Monsieur Agap sowich, that every child here is special. Let us talk about this reasonably. I would like to advocate reason before passion.

What she is, says Mrs Blake – disturbed by Fritz-Peter's beard, his unusually red lips, his too-long eyelashes, what she detects is a very subtle, un-English, un-Scottish, un-Irish accent – is just another child. I will not play favourites – her sharp knuckles whap Monsieur Agapsowich's desk – no matter what the pedigree.

We are paying extravagant amounts of money so that my daughter is treated fairly and taught accordingly, says Louve. Who do you think you are? Give my daughter her toque back.

Louve snaps open her cigarette case. Empty. She forgot.

Mon pays ce n'est pas un pays c'est l'hiver! hums Lai Fun in her toque. She plays the top of her desk like it's a ukulele.

Lou-Anne! Pay attention! shouts Mrs Blake.

French becomes the language Lai Fun associates with leather sandals and rose boutonnieres, men in capes and convertibles, the words "Fuck off" mouthed famously by the devastatingly charming Mr Pierre Elliott Trudeau.

What did he say, daddy?

Fuddle-duddle, Lai Funchen. Fuddle-duddle. Ha ha ha!

Fritz-Peter and Louve laugh their asses off. What a girl!

The French teachers lift and separate her mind like a silky bra on TV, Wonderbra, the delicate white x between her mama's and the TV ladies' boobies; French makes her eyes open wide with Gentilles Alouettes and new, exciting words for even the most banal of things: Soleil. Vert. Joli. Joli joli joli joli joli joli joli joli.

French, a language of elegance. English the language of stasis, the language of Mrs Blake.

Fuddle-duddle. Mrs Blake hates Trudeau with his flowing hair in strange curls around his shoulders and perpetual half-smile that isn't a smile at all, doesn't trust how her breathing hurts when she sees his picture, how her loins leap at the sound of his too-precise voice. *Really* hates him when suddenly, a brand new principal, a *Monsieur* Agapsowich, with an identical haircut, balding on top and the curly flow long past the top of his collar, who wears leather sandals, carries around a ukulele and sings in French and speaks an English so precise it must be foreign. He arrives with a swarm of French-speaking teachers including that dodo Mlle Tremblay – her English so bad – and a swarm of over-privileged brats to start the French programme to "immerse" the children in foreignness. They seduce the other English-speaking teachers, Miss Dranchuck, Mr Kostashuk, into believing Canada is a bilingual country. Canada a country gagging on languages crammed down its throat. People who should know better, like Dina Dranchuk, who listens in on the French singing times and learns the words to "Alouette."

Mrs Blake listens and waits for her day. Fuddle-duddle.

All the kids know that Mrs Blake, head of the English-speaking teachers, silent in her rubber-soled beige shoes, is a monster. All the kids know it. The only ones who don't are the brand new elementaries, and they get to know it fast, especially if their skin isn't white or if their daddies are just a bit too rich or a bit too poor or their mothers a bit too single. In Lai Fun's class, it's Lai Fun, Paul, Kim, Ozzie, Haroun, Lloyd, and Daisy whose dad moved away and whose mom works cashier at the supermarket. The Orange kids.

She sucked the blood out of Mr Smiley, whispers Lai Fun to Daisy. You better watch out. Use your claws like this, she says.

With Ozzie, the first to go, Mrs Blake is gentle and careful. Mrs Blake's mouth fixed on his neck for a little while so she can get the warmest blood, enough to diminish his learning skills. Permanently. Ozzie is the first because Mrs Blake likes to start with the meat and potatoes. She goes on next to Haroun. Lai Fun pees her pants when she sees Mrs Blake latch on to Daisy. Daisy's fingers too soft for claws during silent reading. Mrs Blake rations the rest of the Orange Group because it's rare to find exotic out here on the edge of the prairies where the mountains meet the flatlands, the city so small people still find deer in their backyards and coyotes carry off Patches the kitten or Rags the springer spaniel. Mrs Blake will save Lloyd for last once she figures out how to get past his knuckles – he will be the most delicious because his flesh is prairie, Native, wild, and tangy. Serve with Saskatoon berry sauce.

Mrs Blake. Only those kids whose parents withdraw them

from the school can escape Mrs Hilda Blake's grasp.

Ozzie's problem is that during the first week of school, Ozzie's oilman dad told Mrs Blake no goddamn woman teacher was going to tell him his son wasn't perfect. Mrs Blake resents oilmen with their new money and high falutin' houses in Mount Royal and Eagle Ridge with backyards so humongous coyotes set up dens in them. Mrs Blake hates their cars and boats, hates their trips to Hawaii, and their glittering wives turning tricks downtown for extra cash while the oilmen screw each other in the bathroom at Eaton's. But there have been oil booms before, there are always busts when there are booms. Mrs Blake has seen the history around here. She waits. She waits.

Mrs Blake writes H's on the board, sucks out children's hearts. She sucks out hearts with the grate of her chalk on the board, the snap of her ruler, the flutters of the daisies' white petals on her dress. The rich, the working-class, the ethnics, the ones with the parents who piss her off – she drops into the sink in the teachers' lounge and then turns on the switch of the garburator blades.

Mrs Blake is young, Mrs Blake is pretty. She is the kind of teacher who notices the cut and cost of her pupils' clothes. Who is a judge's kid, who has a single mother who works at a discount clothing store. Which kid has salon-cut hair, which is ruined by a hare-lip, bulgy eyes. What colour the kid's skin is. What the kid's name is: Hadleys fare better than Lai Funs, and Johns excel over Ozzies. In her booming, urban prairie way, Mrs Blake prepares the children for the crappy world out there. Lai Fun learns fast and well that her wiry, tripled pigtails and stupidity around the multiplication blocks that look like small cubes of cheddar cheese don't belong in this class.

Mrs Blake prepares her for the world.

Lai Fun touches an orange block to her tongue. Just plastic.

In June, Mrs Blake watches them when they graduate from Grade One in their paper mortarboards and paper graduation gowns, children lined up single-file to receive their Grade One diplomas because the parents wanted a ceremony. She watches them from the stage-wing, her arms crossed, disgusted at all the pomp and poop for such small, spoiled children. She will always watch them.

CHAPTER 10

Being in a new country like Canada, new cities like Ottawa and Montréal and Calgary and Vancouver and Yellowknife, Louve and Fritz-Peter paying rent and buying bread and tomatoes, staying out at parties past 10:30 PM and not worrying about chaperones, not having parents, grandparents, siblings, aunts, great-uncles, cousins, and half-cousins tracking them in their radar like a wildebeest; finally being treated like adults and not like the babies of their families. Louve can just bang the phone down to end the conversation when one of her viper-sisters tells her she is too old to have a baby. Fritz-Peter can walk inside the house barefooted if he wants. Still the same old ignorance, still stupid Maybelline and Robert and Mrs Blake, but here they have the right to just walk away, they can stretch into the sky, walk in the daylight proudly because they have nothing to be ashamed of, because Canada welcomes everyone. They get vertigo if they look up into the huge, clear skies too long.

The food is different too. It disturbs their stomachs – the meat wilder, tougher, stringier – giving them heartburn and diarrhea. Better to be a vegetarian in the long run.

And the garlic here! How Louve loves the taste of the

garlic, rolls the flavour around on her tongue in sauces, salad dressings, roasted in oil. She makes herself a necklace of garlic, wears it around the house when she vacuums. Garlic. Her new Canadian freedom.

July 1971. Fritz-Peter and Louve go to see the great man, the prototype of the perfect Canadian. Photos of Trudeau on the back of a horse, his wavy hair captured under a white Stetson. They put the photos in an album that holds picture after picture of Louve and Fritz-Peter's Lai Fun, another perfect Canadian who will also speak French, speak English – both languages her first tongues. Lai Fun in the hospital crib right after birth, Lai Fun buried in blankets under the Christmas tree, Lai Fun's first word ("Passion"? or was it "Reason"?), Lai Fun's first puke of solid food, Lai Fun's first birthday, Lai Fun and a shaker of Parmesan cheese. Angélique holding her brand new baby sister Lai Fun during a visit west. Lai Fun's birth announcement, the tag from around her wrist covered in dried, newborn baby goo, and a picture of Pierre Elliott Trudeau on the back of a horse, a sexy St George from Montréal in newly-conquered Canada. The year Pierre Trudeau came to their city.

CHAPTER 11

The Orange Group graduates to high school. Daisy has wasted away, her bones and brain so fragile by the time she leaves Mrs Blake's class, she ploughs through the junior high years, she's too tired to even lift a test-tube in Biology 10. She is beautiful like Karen Carpenter.

Ozzie drifts through the hallways, dumb as a tipped-over cow.

Haroun breaks all his bones in volleyball one afternoon. He tries too hard to make a serve and he breaks his arm in half. The rest of him flips over backward like a jellyfish and he has to go to hospital and lies in traction for six months. His mother tells him to forget the sports and concentrate on becoming an accountant when he leaves university. Accountants don't get their bones broken.

Lai Fun's stomach plops and fizzes into the floor when she walks into the Grade Ten English classroom and there is Mrs Blake, fresh from doing her Master of Education degree at university. Mrs Blake has left elementary school behind, the tentative oasis-from-Mrs-Blake of junior high shattered because Mrs Blake is a senior high school teacher now, Mrs Blake is *Lai Fun's*

Senior High School Language Arts teacher now.

Lloyd gets sent to Monsieur Agapsowich's office for the forty-fifth time when he tells Mrs Blake to, Fuck right off or I'll call the cops.

Lai Fun watches Lloyd stomp away from class, then leans across the aisle to whisper to Daisy.

Mrs Blake's voice anti-freezes, Lai Fun, what is so important you must interrupt the class to tell Daisy?

I was just telling Daisy about the griffins on the Centre Street bridge, says Lai Fun. One of them's about to become a mommy.

One of them's about to become a mommy, repeats Mrs Blake.

That's right, says Lai Fun. The one on the east side of the bridge is pregnant. I noticed her belly on Sunday. I think she's going to lay an egg.

Griffins lay agates, not eggs, says Mrs Blake. What are you? Seven?

The class erupts into a laugh.

When she talked about the griffins fighting on the bridge, the gargoyles doing somersaults on the General Hospital eaves-troughs in her French class, Mlle Laronde told Lai Fun to put them into a short story. Lai Fun got a ten-out-of-ten for her grif-fin and gargoyle story. Even though it wasn't a story, it was the truth. If Lai Fun could, she would silverfish scurry under her desk away from Mrs Blake because Mrs Blake's foot is poised over her, ready to crush her. She listens to the laughing echo around her and through her, bounce off the polished floor, the giant wooden staircases, the wavy-glassed windows, around the walls inside her skull, Mrs Blake's voice, chemical and hateful.

Lai Fun sits in her desk and stares at the first knuckle of her left index finger; she tries not to pee her pants.

Kim Shisamoto is a delinquent pure and true who does any drugs the students from the Gifted Class pass around, drinks so much crème de menthe she has to get her stomach pumped, and regularly has sex with Hank from Regular Grade Twelve in her truck. Lai Fun can't believe it. The sex and drugs part. Just like in the movies. Kim's battle defeats with Mrs Blake have turned Kim into a true slut.

After the griffin episode, Mrs Blake treats Lai Fun like she is a ghost.

Mrs Blake teaches Grade Twelve English as well as English to the Gifted Class kids, the Senior High Yellow Group. Mrs Blake's in charge of Festival Chorus, the Debate Team, Girls' Field Hockey, and wants to be in charge of Stage Band. Mrs Blake is everywhere. The other teachers joke that Mrs Blake has so much time to do so many things because instead of going home she just crawls up the wall to the ceiling and hangs upside down from the school rafters. Her siren-beautiful soprano voice sings along with the chorus and messes everyone up because her voice is so darn loud, and when their school choir comes in twelfth at the Kiwanis music festival, she bawls the whole choir out as spittle flies from her mouth:

You lost because you're beyond lazy! You put on these dresses and feathers and boutonnieres, shuffle around doing a few dance steps that don't look like anything on this earth, and you lot expect that that's going to get you the red ribbon. Well let me tell you, the choir that won has *real* talent and bothered to remember the *words*. Well, we're in the real world now, the real world. You can't spoiled-brat your way to red ribbons.

Lai Fun sits in choir and blanks out the sound of Mrs Blake's voice. All Lai Fun can think about is sex. All she can remember is sex. She knows sex, she believes in sex, and even though no one has ever laid a hand, or a leg, or a sweaty, teenaged, hairy lip on her, she knows all about what it would be like to have sex. One day she will have to have sex. It happens to everybody. Doesn't it? One day a boy will make love to her. And oh yeah, she is gay. She blew it totally when she slipped an anonymous

Valentine's card she made herself into Hadley Constable's desk
and then Lloyd the gonad Weaselhead stole it from Hadley's
desk and waved it around in Home Room shouting out what
Lai Fun had written:

> *Dear Hadley you are the prettiest and most*
> *interesting girl in the school a bright-ringed planet*
> *in the middle of an asteroid field.*
>
> *Signed, A Secret Admirer*

Hadley chortled while Lloyd waved the card around, trying to
guess what boy would be stupid enough to send her an anonymous Valentine's card. Corby Knudsen decided it was Paul so
he gave him a wedgie and nearly squeezed off Paul's balls.

Lai Fun, paralyzed in her seat, tried not to throw up into
her own two hands. She was glad, so glad, she wrote the card
with her left hand to disguise the writing.

Ass stories:

At a party at Stefanja's house that Lai Fun is sure she got
invited to strictly by accident, they all fool around in the snow
in the backyard and Andrew McDonald's hand grabs her ass.
His *hand* on her *ass*. How does she feel about this? She doesn't
know. She wants to put her hand on Hadley's ass.

The first day she wears tight jeans to school, Lloyd shouts:
You've got no ass!

She sits in the seat in front of Morris the evil boy twin in
Math, and he says, Your ass pokes out. You've got a big ass, fuck.

He slaps it with a ruler. And laughs.

Morris slapped her ass! Too bad he's gorgeous. Morris with
eyes like a woman's. She doesn't know what to think of her ass.
It's too big one day, too small the next.

But at least she's not Maureen, who gets called down to
the principal so he can tell her she has to start wearing a bra

because you can practically see her *nipples*. One day in Social before Mr Desjardins comes in, Corby snaps Maureen's bra strap. Lai Fun, in her purple kilt and matching purple sweater her Mama bought her, starts to sweat uncontrollably.

Lai Fun joins Festival Chorus, the Yearbook Committee, and the Dance Committee. Mrs Blake runs them all, but this is just coincidence because Mrs Blake runs everything, there is no getting away from her. No one will dance with Lai Fun at any of the dances. She goes to the Grade Ten Hallowe'en dance as a girl-pirate. She doesn't even dance with her friends because to-night she's resolved she won't until a boy asks her to prove she's normal when all she really wants to do is dance with Hadley Constable, she would die to slip her hands around Hadley Constable's waist the way Lloyd Weaselhead does with his hands on her back, just at the curve leading to Hadley's ass, Hadley' arms around his neck, her head tucked into his shoulder. This is how Lai Fun would like to dance even though that would just be the weirdest thing in the History of the Known World. Trying to slip her hand down on to Hadley Constable's ass.

Hey Ugly, calls Lloyd Weaselhead. That's some hairdo.

This is before she's found him out. She keeps her mouth shut and fusses beside the potato chip machine with the tinfoil sword strapped to her waist.

(Now, well into her thirties, she cannot stand the slow song they played at the end of every dance, "Stairway to Heaven," by big-haired Led Zeppelin. The song that plays when Lloyd shouts at her and Hadley tucks her head even further into his shoulder, *Hey Ugly, that's some hairdo.*)

She works on scenery for school plays with all the drama geeks, Zevon and Vincent and pasty Ozzie in their black jeans and grotty T-shirts. She paints scenery for *Where Are You, Junie Moon?* Because she's part of Festival Chorus, she is automatically one of the singing prisoners in *Man of La Mancha* starring Vincent as the Man and Tomasina as Dulcinea and for sure they're having sex because he's in Grade Twelve and Tomasina has extremely big breasts and gorgeous, long black hair. Vincent can't sing for shit, but he looks like a Man of La Mancha. Tomasina is perfect as Dulcinea, and Haroun plays Sancho Panza even though his parents want him to be an accountant. Haroun is the only one who can actually act, he got the lead in the Grade Eleven French Department production of *Le Misanthrope*.

Louve gives Lai Fun a big bouquet of roses on Opening Night. Lai Fun is only playing the third prisoner from the right. Louve bakes a quiche, Lai Fun's favourite dinner, on Closing Night. Louve goes to the show every night in her bright pink angora sweater and claps the loudest in the audience.

During Lai Fun's Grade Ten year, Fritz-Peter and Louve lose the house. The mortgage rates soar to eighteen percent and when it comes up for renewal, Fritz-Peter tells Lai Fun and her mother to wait for him at Shan Tung restaurant down the street from their house. They eat their dinner – sweet and sour tofu balls! – but don't drive back home to the house that night or any other night.

Fritz-Peter's bowl is full of lai fun noodles and bok choy, but he doesn't eat any of it, just watches Lai Fun eat her rice and sweet and sour sauce. He watches her eat her rice and sauce so closely she doesn't want to eat any more, but she keeps eating, she keeps eating to stop him from saying what he thinks he has to say.

The bank owns the house, Lai Fun, says Fritz-Peter. We'll just stay in a townhouse your mother and I have rented for now, and when the interest rates drop and things sort out, we'll find a newer house. A better house.

During Lai Fun's Grade Eleven year, her father loses his job at the oil company. He is not the only one to lose his job – oil employees across the city and the province lose their jobs too. Angelina Angelini's dad loses his Petro-Canada job; Paul,

Theresa, Ozzie, and David C. at school have parents who work at Petrocan and Chevron and Texaco and Esso and those dads lose their jobs or get told they're going to lose their jobs or they just might lose their jobs, and Louve thanks her lucky stars she still has her nursing job. Fritz-Peter spends his newly free time quietly padding around the rented townhouse dusting the shelves and vacuuming, boiling lentils and chopping up cabbage and grating carrots and frying potatoes for when Louve and Lai Fun get home from work and school. Because he has more time, he begins crocheting parachutes. He thinks about playing golf, which is what his old colleague Boris, who also got laid off, does every day from the second the courses open, but then he changes his mind.

They move again, this time east, to an apartment in Griffins Park – a run-down neighbourhood right next to the train tracks and where the prostitutes hang out close to her school; the hallways of the apartment building smell like cat pee and lemon cleaner, the carpets in the apartment smell like other people's boiled cooking, but her parents tell her this is one apartment they can afford. Everything else is not affordable, as in, *we* can't afford it. Meals at home are affordable; meals in restaurants are not. Staying at home is affordable; Festival Chorus Camp is not. A new Festival Chorus blouse is not affordable; keeping the old one that's getting too small in the boobies is. Taking the train to Vancouver is not affordable, flying to Hawaii for vacation is not affordable, but going to two-dollar-Tuesday movies is. The apartment is closer to Lai Fun's school. That makes walking affordable, whereas a bus pass is not affordable. Louve loses her roses, the giant bleeding-heart bush, with all the moves from house to townhouse to apartment even though she tries to take along clippings in cut-down milk cartons or in plastic sandwich baggies. Luckily, she still has her job.

Fritz-Peter crochets parachutes and knits scarves, darns socks. He makes sauerkraut because cabbage is cheap and nourishing. He makes phone calls and when he's finished making phone calls, he puts on his nicest suit and carries around copies of his resumé in a briefcase.

Mrs Blake smells the Kugelheims' predicament.

Lai Fun asks Mrs Strange the school librarian if she needs a library assistant. Two nights a week, Lai Fun reshelves library books for $3.25 an hour. She likes the library after hours. Ordering the books in neat, decimalled rows, padding softly with her cart full of books down the silent aisles. Once she finds a brain preserved in a jar tucked in behind the books in the non-fiction section and she shows it to Daisy, one of the other Grade Eleven library assistants. Whose brain? Mrs Strange's brain? Lloyd Weaselhead's brain? They scream with laughter. Daisy nibbles at the inside of one of Lai Fun's alfalfa sandwiches while she works. A good sign.

She gives her parents fifteen dollars a month from her library job.

During Lai Fun's Grade Twelve year, Mrs Blake wants to stage *The Mikado*. Even though Lai Fun would automatically be part of the chorus because she is in Festival Chorus in her too-small shirt and they come in fourteenth this time at the Kiwanis music festival and Mrs Blake almost has a brain aneurysm she is so furious, Lai Fun knows it would be fucking unbelievable for a brown girl to dress up like she's Japanese. She doesn't even have to say it; no one asks. She volunteers for wardrobe. She likes costumes even though she finds it difficult to look at the Home Ec. sewing teacher's chapped lips for too long. She can go in after she's done in the library.

But you love singing, says Fritz-Peter.

I don't feel like it. I'll help make costumes. I like costumes.

Well, I'll clap for the costumes.

Thanks, Dad, says Lai Fun.

I have to go to the bathroom, says Lai Fun.

Uh-oh, says Louve.

Lai Fun settles herself on the edge of the bathtub and shaves her legs, armpits, forearms.

You'll only make it grow back thicker, says Louve through the door. Pluck one and ten come to the funeral! That's what happened to your sister and now she's the queen of electrolysis. I, on the other hand, have never shaved.

Her mother's legs covered with invisible wisps.

Oh, says Lai Fun. Too late.

The ritual of soap lather and water and the sharp edge of the metal and rivulets of blood. She rubs deodorant she bought with her own money into her armpits. The gratifying sting on her freshly shaved skin.

Nothing wrong with natural smells, says Fritz-Peter through the door. You've been brainwashed by anti-body propaganda.

Her mother tries the doorknob.

Lai Fun has smartly locked the bathroom door. Continues rubbing on deodorant, lotion, powder. She would like perfume, but she can't afford perfume. She's afraid she'll be smelled by Mrs Blake.

All she wants is to live like everyone else and fit in at school. Swim down the hallways swirling with colognes, anti-perspirants, shampoos, soap, and bodies screamingly clean.

You finally done in the bathroom? asks Louve. Teenage girls and their *toilettes*, eh?

Louve tinkles the ice in her scotch. She wants to call her other daughter Angélique in Montréal and ask for her advice, but the long-distance would be too expensive.

Anyway, as I was saying before you disappeared into the vortex of the bathroom: what about that Mrs Blake? The choir conductor? I really don't like her.

Oh her. She's just crazy, says Lai Fun though the closed door.

I really don't like her. Remember how I told her off when you were in Grade One? Remember? I'll never forget the look on her face! Aha ha ha!

Louve laughs her scotch and cigarettes laugh.

Lai Fun and Daisy the anorexic work in wardrobe for the production of *The Mikado*. No French show this year because the Anglophones have invaded. Lai Fun and Daisy and the Home Economics teacher carefully unpack and unwrap wigs decorated like Mai Tais with plastic flowers and fake jewellery. Lai Fun shakes out the kimonos while Daisy watches from a chair.

Do you think these wigs are real hair? asks Daisy. She leans forward. Puts her pointy chin in her bony hands.

Is this real satin? asks Lai Fun.

I heard that Tomasina says Haroun won't have sex with her, says Daisy. So she says that must mean he's gay. What do you think?

Who's Tomasina? asks Lai Fun. Here, eat my orange. I can't do all these costumes by myself.

Daisy and Lai Fun iron and scorch kimono edges, arrange the hair, ready to freak out if it's real, practise snapping the fans and parasols open and closed and swing their arms in what they think is a regal Japanese way.

Kim Shisamoto is also in wardrobe, her mother wanted her to audition for the actual show – Your voice is so lovely, Kimiko! I heard you in the shower – and Kim thinks her mother is certifiably insane. As bad as the time her mother wanted Kim to dye her hair blonde to play Alice in Wonderland in elementary.

The first day of Lai Fun's wardrobe duty, Kim strides into the music room in her leather jacket and a cigarette tucked behind her ear. She takes a grand sweep of the racks of kimonos, the styrofoam heads holding the floppy black wigs covered in plastic flowers, the fans and parasols and sandals and girls with their carefully white and red and black painted faces and shouts, You've got to be fucking *kidding* me!

Mrs Blake sends Kim to the principal immediately, but he doesn't do anything because even though Kim has the foulest

mouth in the school – boys or girls – Kim's in the French programme merci beaucoup de rien de rien and Kim's mother vis-
its the principal at the drop of one of Kim's cigarettes. Not like
in the old days when parents bowed down so low to the teachers they licked the floors.

Kim pushes away her plate and drinks from her glass of
juice. She stares at her mother. Mom, have you ever seen *The
Mikado*? Kim asks, Do you even know what it's about?

No says Mrs Shisamoto, wiping her mouth with a napkin,
but it's a musical. It's about Japanese people, it's a classic piece
of British musical theatre, the writers Gilbert and Sullivan are
extremely well-known, there was even a movie made about it.

You're clueless.

Kimiko, I am your *mother*. You're three seconds away from
getting expelled and it would help a hell of a lot if you looked
even vaguely interested in extracurricular school activities. You're
way past three strikes, Kimi. If the principal wasn't your father,
you'd be off the baseball field and in prison by now. You will do
this operetta. And I don't want any phone calls from teachers telling me how you didn't show or you showed up drunk.

There's *no fucking way* I'm fucking doing this, Kim's whisper is tight, precise, a clear hiss in Lai Fun's ears. My mother is
sooo mental.

Lai Fun and Daisy cover for Kim because they are a little
scared of her. When Corby Knudsen bowed down in front of
Kim, stuck his top teeth out, and said, Ahhhh sooooo, Mikaaa-
doooo, chop chop! Kim stubbed her cigarette out on his arm.
She stood up to a member of the Trojans football team! Lai
Fun still just turns her head the other way when any of the
Trojans call her by their favourite nickname, Lez Fun. Which
Lloyd Weaselhead started, too stupid to know it was the truth.
Otherwise she is just another chalkboard to them.

The chorus is picked, but the leads need choosing and audi-
tions are held during lunchtime on Tuesday for the girls' parts

and Wednesday for the boys' parts. Three of the Baked Potato People – Hadley, Maureen, and Heather – plus Stefanja Dumanowski, who's also one of the Gifted Class, audition for the roles of the Three Little Maids: Yum-Yum, Pitti-Sing, and Peep-Bo. Zevon, Vincent, and Ozzie plan to audition for the male leads, Nanki-Poo, Ko-Ko, and Pooh-Bah, and casting's in the can until Lloyd finds out that some drama fag is going to actually *touch* Hadley if Hadley gets the part she wants. Lloyd threatens to beat the crap out of Zevon, Vincent, and Ozzie so they suck on purpose. Lloyd and Corby Knudsen, whose mother is a teacher at the school, audition on Wednesday and get the roles of Nanki-Poo and Ko-Ko. None of the Trojans want the drama fags touching their girlfriends, but only Lloyd and Corby are willing to sing in public. Hadley, Maureen, and Heather force another three Trojans to join Festival Chorus, and before the week's out, Trojans and Baked Potatoes run around in wigs and fans and parasols, pretend to sing like they're all teenaged Barbra Streisands.

Stefanja joins the wardrobe group because Mrs Blake told Stefanja it would probably be better for Stefanja to turn down the part of a Maid if she got it because it was only fair that Heather got a chance to be part of the end-of-year show. Heather's dad is the CEO of Fermatron Communications, you know. Stefanja also doesn't shave her legs and this isn't so good. And no one has the guts to tell Lloyd that it's a little bit weird that a Native kid is pretending to be Japanese because he'd football their head and he's so good-looking and popular it really doesn't matter. And Kim just *won't* audition even though her mother has offered to pay a year's worth of insurance on Kim's truck if she does. And Mrs Blake? Mrs Blake has gotten mostly what she wants – Three Little Maids all perfect in size and shape, a Festival Chorus full of young football hunks excellent for the optics. Only Lloyd sticks out, but then, well, Lloyd, Mrs Blake just will have to put up with Lloyd and she chews him out for singing flat and how stupid is he, he can't learn the choreography as fast as everyone else. Closes her eyes and listens to his voice which isn't that bad.

Kim just swears and drinks crème de menthe and smokes and fucks her boyfriend Hank in the back of her uninsured truck, no Little Maid From School is she and after she butts her cigarette out on Ko-Ko's arm, her reputation is complete. Stefanja just shows up one night at rehearsal in the costume room. She combs the wigs and doesn't say much. Her parents are also *not from here*.

Mrs Blake tries to have Kim expelled for butting out on Ko-Ko, but Kim's mother's just married the principal and Mrs Blake has to stop complaining about Kim or risk getting relocated to another school next year because Ms. Shisamoto is both a school trustee and the principal's wife, thank you very much. Kim gets to stay in school, only she has to show up for wardrobe duty for the duration of the play. And help clean the stage every night after rehearsal.

I'd rather be expelled, says Kim, sprawled in the tuba player's chair, her thumbs hooked in her jeans.

Lai Fun and Daisy and Stefanja dutifully comb the wigs back into shape after the dress rehearsal, fold up the hems of the kimonos as the Home Economics teacher pins them into place. Mrs Blake has all the actors and singers stand in a line so she can see the overall effect. The long, uninterrupted pause of powdered white faces with their painted, black, sweeping eyebrows, their bright red button lips. Mrs Blake smiles. The embroidered, imitation satin of the kimonos and the bright flowers on the paper parasols and fans. Bouffant wigs decorated like girly cocktails, and everyone's feet turned in at the correct *Mikado* angles.

Beautiful! exclaims Mrs Blake. Lloyd, more powder! You need to be paler!

Kim shows up with some crème de menthe in a Slurpee

cup and she offers her cup to Daisy and Lai Fun and Stefanja. Daisy says no (her mother's warned her about germs and Kim can't tell her the calorie count), but Lai Fun tries a little because she likes the name. Crème de menthe.

Stefanja takes a sip. It's okay, she says. I'd prefer a whiskey sour.

She pushes the wet mop across the parquet floor of the stage.

Every night before the show, they stitch together kimono rips and glue tiny bits of paper on the holes in the fans, the parasols. Whenever Kim shows up, they do imitations. Daisy does Lloyd singing with his long-necked imitation of a football player being a drama fag, Lai Fun does imitations of Mrs Blake: You can't spoiled-brat your way to red ribbons! she screeches, Red Ribbons! Red Ribbons! and Kim has the prettiest voice of all imitating Hadley imitating an Englishwoman imitating a Japanese woman imitating an Englishwoman: "Here's a How-dee-doo! Here's a How-dee-Doo!" And she does it all after a long drink from her Slurpee cup and a crème de menthey belch. Stefanja sits in the audience and laughs her brains out.

Any of you guys smoke? Kim asks. Too bad for you.

I'll have a puff, says Stefanja.

She takes a long drag of Kimiko's duMaurier King Size. Exhales the smoke from her mouth and sucks the smoke back into her nostrils.

Cigars taste better, she says.

Lai Fun thinks Stefanja's trying too hard. Or maybe she's really a forty-year-old man in a seventeen-year-old body.

On closing night just before the show, Lai Fun kneels onstage and tries to glue closed a hole in one of the paper screens. She kneels and cuts and glues and while she is cutting and gluing she sees Lloyd Weaselhead and Corby Knudsen walk backstage.

They play-wrestle for a while. Lloyd punches Corby on the

shoulder and then Corby leans forward and kisses Lloyd. Lloyd kisses him back and then they are all grabbing asses, tongues in each other's mouths. Lai Fun shouts through the curtain, Hey Lloyd! Why doncha just get a hotel room! and Corby bolts while Lloyd stands there, his hands trembling.

Ugly! says Lloyd, because he has to be king of the upper hand even though she's found him out and he knows it. Lai Fun goes back to her screen. She kneels and glues and cuts and glues and wipes and Lloyd Weaselhead comes up behind her, she can smell him, his boy cologne, his hair gel, his lusty sweat and saliva, and he's probably going to pulverize her but she doesn't care, why should she care about anything any more, she has never fit, she will never fit, she is Ugly, a kind of harmless monster, she comes from a family of monsters. She will receive at Lloyd's hands what monsters like her always receive, then she will slither away to her hole and the curtain will come down.

He touches the tip of her ear. She freezes.

You tell anyone, Lloyd whispers, and I'll burn down your fucking house.

It's no big deal, Lloyd, she says. She turns around and looks at him and she is sweating so hard she can feel the sweat eating through the cloth in her armpits, through the crotch of her pants. She can smell the chemicals in her menstrual pad (that's the last time she's buying the deodorant ones, sale or no sale!).

I'm just saying you should be more discreet, she says.

You tell anyone, he says, and I'll spread it around the school that you're a big lez.

She stands up. What are you? Seven? *You're* the lez, Lez Weaselhead. It's so *obvious*. And I really don't care. So what if I like girls? So what?

She crosses her arms.

Really? I was just kidding.

You're always kidding.

When did you get so tough? says Lloyd.

You're a goober, too stupid to know that he shouldn't kiss his boyfriend in public and expect to live. I won't tell anyone.

You won't?

I won't tell, Lloyd. I have other things to worry about.

All right.

All right.

Right.

Yes.

No one. You won't tell Hadley, says Lloyd. You *swear*.

Go away, Lloyd.

Thanks, Lez.

She gasps when he hugs her, kisses her cheek, then runs out the door.

Lloyd, her new best friend. Her first kiss.

The male chorus stomps their way through the opening number, they stamp and clap and snap their fans, "If you want to know who we aaaaare!," they sing, "We are gentlemen of Japaaaaaan!" Their eyebrows jumping across their foreheads, their lips red blossoms. Lloyd, the wandering Nanki-Poo minstrel, wanders in Stage Right with his second trombone. No one's hands on Hadley Yum-Yum but his now. No one's hands on Corby but his.

Lai Fun stands with Stefanja, Kim, and Daisy backstage among the costumes. Lai Fun and Stefanja and Daisy tie ribbons, fasten kimonos, bobby-pin giant wigs onto scalps, hunt for misplaced fans. Little Maids from Titipu all in a frenzy, tittering quietly before their entrance. Kim stands outside behind the building, smoking and smoking and kicking a concrete meridian in the parking lot waiting for this stupid show to finally be *over* and her life to get back to *normal*. The female chorus swishes onto stage with their parasols and ribbons; Hadley, Heather, and Maureen trill through "Three Little Maids" in partial harmony, giggle behind their parasols, and scamper away Stage Left. Mrs Blake notices that even on closing night they still haven't managed to remember to keep their toes turned inward, but oh well.

Nanki-Poo and Ko-Ko enter Stage Right and begin to sing. Mrs Blake closes her eyes and listens to Corby and Lloyd's voices, the notes' swift twinning and flowering. She sighs. A scent whispers past her nose, but it must just be their voices, of course it is the music.

Lai Fun, Stefanja, and Daisy, in a cloud of hairspray and talcum powder, sneak outside and take turns kicking meridians with Kim.

Lai Fun tries Kim's cigarette and coughs and coughs and adores the corruption of the lungful of smoke. She in-in-in-hales. Feels her head spin on the teapot ride at the Stampede. In a moment of solidarity, Kim and Daisy and Lai Fun and Stefanja all exchange phone numbers even though Daisy and Lai Fun are still a little scared of Kim. Stefanja thinks she's just a poser, it's *sooo* obvious. Lai Fun, in a tizzy from the smoke and the crème de menthe, stares happily at the stripe of blue on Daisy's brown polyester shirt that she seems to wear every second day at least, and breathes in Daisy's lotiony, powdery smell, Kim's rough leather jacket, and the comforting stink of cigarette smoke because the smell reminds Lai Fun of her parents.

I love the way you smell, says Lai Fun to Daisy, and she takes another happy puff from one of Kim's duMaurier King Size cigarettes.

The girls laugh outside in the cold, in the cigarette smoke, around the crème de menthe. Then toss away the cup and the cigarettes and walk inside.

Onstage, Hadley sits in a pool of spotlight and gazes at herself in a hand-mirror. An artificial cherry tree in full bloom arches over and little maids swirl around her like confetti. She looks up at the audience, then back down at the mirror. She strokes the lock of wig hair tossed forward over her shoulder. "Sometimes I sit and wonder," says Hadley, her voice bouncing off the theatre walls and ceilings, "in my artless Japanese way, why it is that I am so much more attractive than anybody else in the world."

A little too much like real life and Lai Fun, Stefanja, Kim, and Daisy's laughs batter the walls and Mrs Blake in the audience turns bright red from fury, the sound of laughing from backstage while the show is on. Girls. Hysterical teenage girls; Kim is already a lost cause heading to nowhere. And the other three – Mrs Blake will take care of them. Lai Fun she will take care of in a way no mother can leap in and protect. Girls are easily ruined when friendships go wrong, especially girls like Lai Fun with their vulnerable hearts.

At the closing-night party, the band master and Mrs Blake put out cups of pop and bowls of chips for all the singers.

Please put away your wigs and costumes in an orderly manner, calls Mrs Blake and of course the singers, some with giant bouquets of lilies and roses, ignore her because the salt from the chips, the liquid sugar in the pop already start to hype them up, but for once Mrs Blake doesn't care because the show was a success. In spite of the failed harmonies and crooked feet and the strange smell emanating from Corby and Lloyd whenever they were onstage together.

Stefanja pins wigs to the styrofoam heads while Kim watches. Lai Fun walks onto the stupid stage where she's glad she didn't have to sing and collects fans and socks and paper flower petals. Daisy sweeps in untidy circles.

Lloyd Weaselhead kissed me! says Lai Fun out of the blue, into the empty room of the auditorium.

He did? Lloyd Weaselhead is such a spaz.

Lai Fun can't believe Daisy just called Lloyd a spaz. Was it spaz-like for him to kiss her on the cheek? If Lloyd is a spaz, he's the most famous spaz in the school.

Can he kiss? asks Daisy.

Wha-what?

Can he kiss? Is he a good kisser?

I don't know.

Daisy stares.

You said he kissed you!

He kissed me on the cheek.

Why would he kiss you? Are you lying? Why does he call you Ugly all the time if he's kissing you in private?

No, it was a friendly kiss. I can't tell you why. I'm not lying. Why would I lie?

Oh Lai Fun, says Daisy, You wouldn't know a kiss from a friend from a kiss from a lover, and Daisy gives Lai Fun a great big kiss on the lips. She holds Lai Fun's face in her hands and her lips and breath taste of mint, Daisy's face soft and bony and perfect like the rose in Trudeau's lapel, and Daisy's fingers burning. The accidental clink of Daisy's teeth against Lai Fun's because Lai Fun's mouth was open while her lips were forming the word "lie."

Lezzies, says Kim from the Stage Left wing. I'm hanging out with lezzies. Hilarious.

Lloyd wasn't lying when he called you a lez in Social? asks Stefanja. She pops her head from behind the curtain, a mannequin's head covered with a giant wig in her hands. I thought he was just making it up. Tell me he was making it up.

I am not a lezzie! shouts Lai Fun.

It's no big deal, says Kim. It's just a word. Stop being such a blow-job.

Blow-job, Daisy laughs.

Lai Fun in the bathroom cubicle, sitting on the edge of the toilet, her hands in her lap. She is a lezzie. In name *and* in body. She wishes she could talk to Lloyd.

Mrs Blake makes it very easy for Daisy's father to pick Daisy up that last day at school even though she knows he doesn't have visitation rights. But it's one less student for her to worry about. Daisy hesitating, then disappearing into the back of the taxi cab with her father, never to be seen again. Daisy's distraught mother comforting Mrs Blake, telling Mrs Blake it wasn't her fault, she couldn't have known how ruthless Daisy's father could be, that Daisy's dad had been trying to get Daisy back for a year and a half.

Daisy's face a Missing Person poster in the bus station.

Lai Fun sits in Language Arts, her head a hole in the top of her neck and for old time's sake, because Grade Twelve graduation is around the corner, Mrs Blake gives Lai Fun a detention for drawing black cubes with her leaky ball-point pen all over the cover of her binder instead of writing a Reflection on *The Old Man and the Sea*.

Lai Fun sits in her desk, blank paper in front of her trying to care about the old man, the sea, and the big fish. Mrs Blake looks up from her stack of marking every so often and watches Lai Fun, Lai Fun's chewing her own fingers, Lai Fun the lezzie chewing her bleeding cuticles.

Mrs Blake sighs, then stands up. She walks to Lai Fun, puts her hand in the bend between Lai Fun's neck and shoulder, and squeezes hard.

I have all day, Lai Fun, she says. And all night.

Lai Fun sits, paralyzed, and as she walks back to her desk, Mrs Blake secretly sniffs her fingers. Lai Fun won't tell her parents because they won't believe her. They stopped believing anything she said back in Grade One. She puts her pen to the paper and begins to write about old fish.

Why so mopey? asks Fritz-Peter. Boyfriend didn't call? He sets placemats on the table, then plates and glasses.

No. I mean – I don't have a boyfriend.

Good. A pretty girl like you, says Louve, chopping up onions and garlic. You don't want to get ahead of yourself. Better to get a degree and a job first. Then you can think about boys. Can you find me some matches? I've run out and I would like to light a candle for the dinner-table. You're getting thin. You aren't eating enough.

Lai Fun slides open the balcony door, goes outside, and picks the matchbook off the small patio table. She flips open the matchbook. The matchbook is empty. She looks in the turtle-shaped box by the television for the matches. She looks in her mother's purse for matches. She starts to cry.

What's wrong? If you can't find matches, go find your daddy's lighter. It's in the bedroom.

I want to be like other people.

What?

Lai Fun sobs.

Fritz-Peter comes from the bathroom where he's been reading *The National Enquirer* and trying to scrape car grease out from under his fingernails. Why is the Noodle crying? he asks.

Louve takes her cigarettes out of her purse.

She says she wants to be like other people, says Louve.

Why is this something to cry about? asks Fritz-Peter. You'd better use a Kleenex.

Dinner will be ready in forty-five minutes. Why do you want to be like other people? It would be different if we were in Ottawa. In Ottawa, things were happening every night, people dressed like their lives depended on it. They couldn't help being interesting because they were in Ottawa. And when Ottawa got boring, we'd just cross the bridge to Hull.

Well, says Fritz-Peter, it's much better than when we first moved here. Back then there were only four cinemas. None of them played on Sundays. You couldn't drink beer in your own back yard because it was against the law. There we were, drinking beer out of coffee mugs. Like barbarians. We chased gas flares for entertainment!

I don't know why you gave birth to me, says Lai Fun. I didn't ask to be born.

Louve puts down the cigarettes.

Honey, we wanted you, she says.

That is not a logical statement, Fritz-Peter interjects. Who is ever asked if he wants to be born? No one ever asked anyone if he wanted to be born.

It's not fair. If we can't be like other people, why don't we move somewhere else?

Should we have sent you a telegram when you were in your mother's womb? Ha ha ha!

It's because of that Mikado play, isn't it? asks Louve.

Louve smokes and smokes and smokes. She gets up and puts Cat Stevens on the turntable. Plops down on the couch and stares out the window.

Lai Fun shouts over "Peace Train": I'm going to change my name!

Lord, give me faith and patience, says Louve.

A name people think is normal. Like Faith or Patience. Everyone thinks I'm some sort of fucked up Chinese woman!

We really like Lai Fun, says Fritz-Peter, setting forks and plates on the table, stirring vegetables in the wok on the stove. It's my favourite kind of noodle. Also it's an expensive process, changing your name. You'd be paying for it yourself, you know. Your mother and I wouldn't help you pay.

Gawd! says Louve.

I'm changing my name to Jane.

You know what? I'm too tired for this. *Jane.*

Lai Fun turns to leave the room.

I don't know why children can't tell when they're breaking their parents' hearts, says Louve. She leans forward and taps her cigarette on the edge of the ashtray. My sister's name is Jane. Why not Louise? Like Louise Lasser from *Mary Hartman, Mary Hartman*?

Who in the world asks to be born? asks Fritz-Peter. Louise Lasser had a drug problem.

I'm tired of being the weird-looking, weird-named immigrant kid, says Lai Fun.

Louve refuses to cry in front of Lai Fun. No, she must protect her vulnerable heart because an unprotected heart only leads in one direction. She cries in front of Fritz-Peter though, in the night she sobs her heart out because her daughter is becoming *one of them* and there is nothing Louve can do about it. They should never have moved here. They never should have.

Lai Fun goes to her room, sits in the corner by the closet, and puts a paper Safeway bag over her head. Fritz-Peter finishes setting the table. Louve lights the candle with the lighter from the bedroom. She spoons fried eggplant and garbanzo beans and mashed garlic potatoes onto the plates, pours out orange juice.

Lai Fun wanders like a wisp of smoke into the room and pulls out her chair at the dinner table.

Fritz-Peter notices the marks over the eggplant shepherd's pie.

Big hickey on your neck, eh Lai Fun? When do we get to meet him? I want to ask him if he is prepared to support you in the manner to which you have become accustomed. Ha ha ha!

What? Living in a flea-bag apartment with hallways that stink of cat piss? It's not a hickey. Fuck off, Dad.

Silence drops in the middle of the table and bursts like a bag of garbage.

Don't you ever, *ever* speak to your father that way, Lai Fun, says Louve.

That's fine when you're with your friends, but I take offense when you tell me to fuck off. What is on your neck?

Fritz-Peter thumbs Lai Fun's collar away from her neck.

Leave me alone! Lai Fun turns red and her armpits run with sweat from all the looking and the poking.

Noodle! shrieks Louve. Who made these fingerprints?

A boy. Just like Dad said. His name is Lloyd Weaselhead.

Louve, says Fritz-Peter. These are not hickeys.

These are not hickeys, Lai Fun. Who did these? Tell me the truth.

Mrs Blake did them. I told you she does things like that. I told you a long time ago.

I'm phoning the principal, says Fritz-Peter. Mrs Blake. We have to phone the principal.

I'm going to the school, says Louve. Oh my god. Where's my purse?

Louve's hands shake as she bumbles with her coat.

Fritz-Peter, you stay with Lai Fun. Where's my purse? I can't find my keys! I can't find my glasses!

Lai Fun. Lai Fun, my little girl, sighs Fritz-Peter. I guess we should have telegrammed you for permission.

Fritz-Peter sits down beside Lai Fun. Pats her awkwardly on the shoulder.

Your breath stinks, says Lai Fun.

Lai Fun sits on the floor in her room with her plate on her lap and her glass of orange juice beside her. Ever since Lloyd Weaselhead kissed her cheek, ever since Daisy kissed her lips then disappeared, Lai Fun's heart has not stopped weeping. She remembers Lloyd Weaselhead as her first twin and sometimes when she lays her head on her desk she hears the slow shifting of a Daisy-flower inside her brain but doesn't know what it means. Daisy? Who's Daisy?

Lai Fun is not a girl, she is a haunted house. She has a broken heart and all people with broken hearts are haunted. She has a condemned building for a heart and so her heart does what all distressed buildings do: it implodes like a worn-out hospital, like a used-up, sandstone school.

In the morning, Mrs Blake is replaced by a substitute teacher, Mr Piano, who tells Lai Fun that Mrs Blake must have taken Lai Fun's Reflection home with her, so he has no idea what Lai Fun's grade on the Reflection is, if she wants, he'll just put down an A-. Mrs Blake isn't a chaperone at the Grade Twelve graduation dance, but Lai Fun hardly notices. She is too busy hiding among the clusters of green and white balloons.

PART III

---·◆·---

THE WAY OF
THE SUBURBS

CHAPTER 12

The way of the suburbs.

Lai Fun, her wife Jennifer Singh, and Lai Fun's older sister Angélique are Stefanja's neighbours in those airy, cedar-sided houses in the southwest part of the city. They are the only lesbians on the street and when other neighbours point out their house, look out their windows at the house, the neighbours say, That's the Lesbians' House. Stefanja and Lai Fun are old French immersion school chums and, twenty years later, kitty-corner neighbours! And now that Lai Fun's older sister Angélique has moved into Lai Fun's basement and agreed to be a nanny for Freddy, Lai Fun's life is ordered like a Rolodex and Stefanja can take a few extra work days because Angélique babysits Olivia too. Angélique serenades Freddy and Olivia with her ukulele playing. She started ukulele lessons six months ago.

Poor, tortured Stefanja Dumanowski. Stefanja's husband Thor says he would rather be gutted alive with pliers than go to his own high school reunion, so why would he go to hers? He writes at home while Stefanja writes up schedules for step class, swimming, yoga, and squash instructors at the Leisure Centre. She prints signs that say Please Remove Your Street

Shoes and No Black-Soled Shoes On The Courts.

Thor puffs on his asthma ventilator to open his lungs a little bit, then lights up a joint. Stef would have a cow: Not in front of the baby! Stefanja always says, but the baby's been asleep for hours. Not even a baby any more, but a stumbling, disorderly mini-Stefanja. Thor buys an extra bag of weed to celebrate the arrival of Angélique.

Thor pours himself another glass of wine to get the creative juices flowing. Scrubs at his hair with his hands and looks at the shower of dandruff that falls on the keyboard of his computer, the hard, dark wood of the desk. Maybe he will go clean out the eavestroughs.

Thor is smart and he is hungry for success, but the truth is he's not smart enough to be a chain-smoking, high-functioning alcoholic *and* a great writer. He is not the next Quentin Tarantino, video-clerk-makes-good-as-mega-Hollywood-director, because Thor would never work as a videoclerk. Although Thor is still very good at making commercials: panning Aisle Two in "Family's Groceteria," then cutting to close-ups of garbage bags and duck-shaped toilet cleansers. Thor is a talented artist balancing a wife, a baby, and a gorgeously pregnant lesbian mistress, although he would never use the word "mistress" in front of Lai Fun again (he did once and she put on her clothes and left). He is a brilliant rake, a Mozartian rogue, when he writes more than one draft. When he isn't telling everyone and their twenty-five cent feeder fish about his latest idea for a script before the script is even a quarter of the way through its first draft – talking his ideas about Mafia heists and extraterrestrials and Vietnam scenarios into the ground and giving advice about how to snag agents and film deals and contracts.

He isn't going to Stefanja's dumb reunion. He wouldn't go to her parents' fortieth wedding anniversary, he has never gone to any of her office Christmas parties. He is very protective of himself being exposed to the banal kind of individual who attends

Christmas potlucks and parents' wedding anniversaries and reunions and book clubs who might pollute his creativity. He is
a *writer*. He resisted meeting Lai Fun and her lover for years
no matter how much Stefanja told him they wouldn't pollute
him, they would inspire him – they were so sophisticated, they
made buckets of money in the information technology industry. Then eight months ago, he looked up from his computer
and out the window, watched Lai Fun getting out of her car
after work on a Friday afternoon in an unusually clingy, knitted
top that showed the points of what he sixth-sensed were delec-
table nipples. He suddenly realized she was a *lesbian*.

That weekend over the steamy bowl of Lai Fun's vegan
bouillabaisse, Thor smelled Lai Fun's crotchy heat. When Stefanja got up to go to the kitchen, he looked at Lai Fun. She
sneered at him. Stefanja came back from the kitchen giggling
as she put the dessert, Sex in a Pan, on the table. Stefanja left to
close up the gym and said she'd be back in thirty minutes; Jennifer called and said sorry she'd missed dinner, she'd be home as
soon as she could, save her some pan-sex; and Lai Fun pushed
Thor onto the floor. The children slept under their crocheted
blankets in Freddy's room.

This is the way of the suburbs.

Thor's problem, Stefanja believes – although she would
never say – is that he talks too much. He talks and talks and
talks so that all the air leaks out of his pretty blockbuster movie
balloons. And Stefanja knows he's fucking some dumb bitch
who doesn't tell him to put away his Hollywood dream and
concentrate on making the best Pete the Plumber commercials a human could possibly make – his floozie doesn't care
about practicalities. Floozie probably looks at the cover page
of his latest screenplay and gets screamingly wet because she
wants his artist's brain so bad. Stefanja knows artists' brains
also have to feed and clothe their families and even though his
screenplays also sometimes-occasionally-once-in-a-while make

her wet, she pushes Thor into commercials and production assistant jobs for movies-of-the-week – not because she doesn't appreciate his artistic vision, but because she truly loves him. Thor needs guidance, that's all.

Thor's parents think he is a gift to the world, and when he sends them his screenplays, they say: You're wasting yourself in such a small town – move to New York! Move to L.A.! Our son the genius. His mother plots how she can run away with Thor to Los Angeles like eloping lovers and she can escape Thor's lump of a father.

Stefanja drags him down.

Stefanja has stopped agreeing with him when he mentions how famous he could be.

You're brilliant, said Stefanja in his final year at film school.

Now she flips through his screenplays and makes her judgment in fifteen minutes instead of spending the *days* she used to spend loving his work.

Yes, I am, he said, his thick fingers up her shirt and down her underpants, his sea slug of a tongue wedged in her left ear.

And she melted into tears at her own sweet luck. His body thick and hot. They necked in his parents' sitting room in the shadow of his trophies for most promising student and best film of the year. She was so lucky, a blonde bear of a man. To die for. The oh-so-blonde man of her dreeeeeams.

Thor Thor Thor.

Now she unloads the dishwasher with a clatter when he tells her about yet another script he's started about yet another Mafia heist gone wrong.

I'm sorry, she says. Can you start over again? The dishes and the running water were making too much noise.

Thor, honey. It's really good, but hasn't that been done already? Hasn't it been done a million times?

She changes Olivia's shirt, then changes it again when Olivia splats Cream of Wheat *under* her bib. She scrubs down the kitchen counter, which is covered in crumbs. Cream of Wheat and crumbs and baby spit in her hair so dirty she could twist sculptures into it.

But telling Thor his ideas are as brilliant as Cream of Wheat under a bib hurts his feelings.

So she blinks her giant hazel eyes and smiles at him as though he is still her brilliant fiancé and not her husband of years and years who's doing some other woman on the side. Which is perhaps worse than the other comment she doesn't make about Cream of Wheat brilliance. He must think she is stupid not to know he is seeing another woman. She would like to shout, The least you could do is shower, you know! – but that would disturb their household's steamy dishwasher calm, the baskets of carefully-folded Thor laundry, the shovelled walk, the changed light bulbs. Because Thor may be a lug and a lousy writer, but at least he can lift things and put up Christmas lights. Stefanja would have to contemplate divorcing him and living a life of cleaning dead squirrels out of the chimney flue by herself, for example. So instead she does nothing. Nothing keeps Thor and his cookie-cutter Mafia stories out of her Cream of Wheat hair. Nothing keeps Stefanja and Thor and Olivia and the chimney flue clean and precise.

Stefanja scoops clumped cat pee from the litter box. Bounces Olivia up and down up and down on her lap with a jingly toy for cats she bought to try to get Olivia to *stop screaming*. She looks out at the identical houses on the too-quiet street.

This is the way of the suburbs.

Lai Fun married to Jennifer Singh who used to be a receptionist at Gargoyle but who became the new boss in her tailored suits and English accent getting her MBA degree and playing golf with the right people, and joining book clubs with the right people even though Jennifer Singh only reads *Report on Business* and the business sections of both national newspapers. Jennifer Singh making Lai Fun tag files and hunt for the ends on rolls of scotch tape instead of running her sub-section which is what Lai Fun is trained to do. Slipped in right when Lai Fun wasn't looking, right when she thought the job Jennifer Singh got was a cookie for Lai Fun to eat. Her partner and colleague, once upon a time the cute, overly ambitious receptionist, now suddenly her spouse and a supervisor at the head office downtown. As her supervisor Lai Fun could fucking kill Jennifer Singh who memos the office silly and holds meetings once a week like no one has any real work to do – as her partner she is clean and efficient and never home which drives Lai Fun to have sex with the dolt next door. Lai Fun never sees Jennifer except at work, at her desk diddling on the computer, on the phone, at the head of the table in the boardroom ordering sub-committee after ad hoc committee after super-committee. The last time they had sex was at the office eight months ago when Jennifer wanted to celebrate the brand new contract with Headley Waterstone's company, wanted to crack open a bottle of champagne. Lai Fun just wanted some goddamn sex with her wife for once in a decade and suggested they drink the champagne, have sex, and have another baby.

Lai Fun roughly kissing and sucking at Jennifer's throat, her nipples, her naked shoulders, just like in those foreign movies that come on Channel 32 after eleven o'clock. As she sucks, she wonders why in the world she can't find a more creative solution to her need to get off than with Stefanja's stupid husband. Jennifer Singh, who will only allow herself to be touched every eleven-and-a-half months. Why in the hell does Jennifer Singh think a job is more sexually exciting than Lai Fun? What kind of example is Lai Fun setting for the baby in her uterus – the witness to Lai Fun's zillions of transgressions? Why are her pregnancy hormones doing this to her? Why does this baby insist on being such a goddamn voyeur and embryonic pornographer?

The baby must be the High Lord Executioner of Lai Fun's hormones.

Lai Fun and Jennifer Singh are two professionals with one baby named Frederick, another one on the way, and two cars even though they work at the same place. Thor hungry for Lai Fun's growing moonscape of a body when he isn't stupid from dope (I want to put your pregnant navel into one of my screenplays, he says, and Lai Fun flushes, suddenly she really needs to pee).

So Stefanja says your mother's trying to write a book? says Thor one afternoon after musty sex. He lights up a joint. Maybe I could mentor her.

But Lai Fun's too busy peeing hard and she needs to shower his stink off *now*.

This is the way of the suburbs.

Stefanja hires Angélique as a babysitter.

Wednesday afternoon, Stefanja calls in sick at work and she and Angélique take the kids to the zoo. There in the dinosaur park, Stefanja asks Angélique nosey questions because she's bored and because she can and because Angélique never ever shocks, never asks questions back.

Why do you always wear black? asks Stefanja.

Hides the dirt, says Angélique.

Did you always know you were a lesbian or did you figure it out later?

I knew from the second my father's sperm penetrated my mother's egg.

How old are you?

Guess.

You look twenty-two, but I know that can't be right. Fifty-four?

Angélique turns and looks at Stefanja, Angélique's lips plastic-glossy with lipstick. Fifty-four, she says. That's right. And her mouth tics into a smile. She resumes pushing Freddy's stroller.

So what did you do when you lived in Montréal? asks Stefanja, her cheeks red from the cool rush of the wind.

I was a lawyer.

You gave up all that money?

I was laid off, says Angélique.

Does that bother you?

I manage. Angélique ties her head scarf tighter under her chin.

How can I get my husband to stop taking me for granted?

Love isn't immortal, sighs Angélique.

Stefanja sighs back. Maybe she doesn't want all the answers.

This is the way of the suburbs.

CHAPTER 13

It wasn't just that Angélique's law firm laid her off, it was that Montréal kicked her out. Even though she had been living there for almost ever, Montréal rejected her like a bored lover. She remembers the day she sat at her desk in her office, her blue fountain pen in her hand. The pen exploded all over her fingers, her papers. Angélique sat in her office, contemplated the puddles of ink, and wondered if she should buy an expensive dinner or cut her throat. She dabbed at the mess with half a box of tissue, then gathered up her briefcase and coat and walked out of the building to the metro station. She waited in the calm blue and grey of the tunnel, smelled the heat of the tracks, the perfume and sweat of the other commuters. Her body gone so tight all over – her skin, her gums, her fingernails, her ears – her body no longer hers. She'd forgotten what the sky looked like. She lived her clients' lives, made their litigious neighbours and miserly dead aunts her business, then the firm laid her off and her pen exploded.

Her girlfriend Marguerite, the five-foot-eleven-and-a-half poet who was allergic to nuts, was going to dump her anyway. Angélique could tell from the three weeks of pasta every single night. Marguerite only ever made pasta when she was depressed because Marguerite believed that it was physiologically impossible to be sad while eating pasta. Angélique could taste the sadness not only in the noodles themselves, but in the pecorino cheese sprinkled on top of the elaborate, depressing sauces. The sauce's sadness more shocking than the entire cloves of garlic pretending to be pieces of potato. Tasted the sadness in Marguerite's armpits, even in the small of her back when they made love, the only time they talked and then only in monosyllables, sex and pasta all the time and nothing else.

Her last month. In her office, she pressed the remote to resume hour seven of the videotape her client, soon to be someone else's client, had given her. Property line dispute. The tape, her client assured Angélique, held definite proof of harassment and conspiracy. This part of the tape was 3:40 AM. The neighbour's house dark. Angélique watched the dark house full of probably sleeping people. She wondered what she should cut her throat with. A letter opener, a ballpoint pen, the corner of her desk? Whether she'd prefer a restaurant close to work or the better ones closer to home.

Sleeping and harassing? Come on!

Angélique left Montréal to go west. She lost her job, she lost her girlfriend, her heart marinated in pesto and sprinkled over day-old pasta salad. The decline began with her law degree, which drained away her imagination and wanted her mind to be so narrow she could look through a keyhole with both eyes. Then it was the man who bawled his eyes out during Discovery – he cried so hard when Angélique asked him to give his name he couldn't speak and his own lawyer hadn't thought to bring Kleenex, so Angélique gave him some from her pocket and she knew she was sunk, she cared about the client she'd been hired to sue and watching videotapes of this man asleep in his house was probably the silliest job a human being could do and still get paid for. Then Marguerite with her pasta depression and nut-allergy garlic-crushed Angélique's heart and the nadir of Angélique's existence splashed up into her face from the toilet bowl of life at a women's-only birthday party when she watched a Topless Twister game featuring Marguerite getting it on with whomever Marguerite could get her hands on. Right foot on green! Left breast on yellow! Marguerite twisting and contorting her body so that everyone in the room could see her naked breasts. The depressed pasta smell had stopped surrounding Marguerite; for the first time in too long Angélique noticed Marguerite only smelled that way when Marguerite was alone with *her*.

At the party Angélique helped light the candles, light the barbecue, the pilot light on the old gas stove. She lit the tea warmer, women's cigarettes, the incense sticks in the bathroom. She lit the leg of a chair without thinking about it, then ran to the kitchen for water, for baking soda to douse the flame. She could light everything but Marguerite's heart.

Six months later, she moved west like a homesteader, moved to the same city as her sister, her parents. Angélique wanted to hear Louve call her "my baby"; she wanted to spend time with her little nephew and, soon, the new baby. Living with Lai Fun and her family as a nanny to Freddy. Her education never prepared her for a younger sister and her babies, but she wanted to learn about diaper-rash and colic, how to live like a monk, a nun. Celibate and pure.

Since the Topless Twister game, she realized she was too old and that she should just get a cat and name it something pretentious and clever like Kim Campbell, Pitti-Sing, or Una Crayon. Or take up a musical instrument, the tuba, the French horn, something she had wanted to do since she went to one of Lai Fun's elementary school ukulele concerts in the seventies. And move west. If she could, she would just burn down Montréal, along with the rest of her past, then flee to a quiet dinner.

Angélique pushes Freddy in his stroller past identical lawns, identical picture windows in the relentless sun that shines even in forty degrees below zero. The wheels of the stroller twist and trundle and Freddy sits calmly with his hands on his knees, his head soft as a baby duck's.

See, Freddy? House. Lawn. House. Lawn. Grass. Say it! Grass!

Grass! says Freddy, Mawn! Mouse!

Freddy's hands in his lap, his face wrinkled and happy. He listens to the swish of Angélique's long black skirt, the clump of her big black boots. Her laid-off-lawyer, freshly-dumped-lover outfit makes her look like a vampire, but she doesn't care, and when people are rude enough to stare or ask her why she's so dressed up, she says she's from Montréal.

Dog, she says. Car. Dog poo. Bus. Bowling alley. Overflowing garbage can. The Rose Café – yay!

Yay! says Freddy and he raises both hands into the air.

Angélique wheels him in through the front door and orders a chamomile tea because any other drink just makes her heart beat too fast when she thinks about what yesterday was like and what tomorrow will undoubtedly bring. She unpacks Freddy's sippy cup full of Special Freddy Juice they whipped up together in the blender (along with some raw carrots she sneaked in while Freddy chased a grape fallen to the floor) because Freddy loves watching the blender. She wheels him to face her and locks the wheels of the stroller. Her nephew drinks his juice. She gives him his scribbling book and his Gumby toy and opens her own book, *Wray: The Life of Fay Wray*.

Everything peachy until she gets home and hears a message on the answering machine: "Angélique. It's me." Marguerite, soon to be in town for her twenty-year high school reunion.

CHAPTER 14

Lai Fun can't believe Daisy's in town all the way from Montréal. She can't believe Daisy's in town for the twenty-year reunion when she didn't even phone Daisy, Daisy found it on the school alumni website, Daisy said she *looked* for the reunion. She can't believe Daisy's in town and that Daisy is also one of Angélique's ex-girlfriends except in Montréal her name is Marguerite, her father's family always called her Marguerite, Daisy in French is Marguerite, how obvious. What a soap opera! Lai Fun should be on Angélique's side because Angélique is her sister and Daisy/Marguerite dumped Lai Fun's sister and what about blood loyalty? On the other hand, *Daisy's* in town for the reunion *Lai Fun* organized.

Invite her for dinner the night before the reunion, says Lai Fun. Please. I'll cook, even.

She *dumped* me, says Angélique. She's also allergic to nuts. All you eat is nuts practically.

Angélique putters with the dishes in the kitchen sink. Freddy clings to her leg and hums. Ecstatic to be with his auntie. As usual.

Well, I need my protein. Come here, Freddy, says Lai Fun. Freddy, come *here*.

And she grabs his hand and hugs him to her.

Grab a steak then, says Angélique. Go suck on someone's neck. Ha ha ha!

You should be friends, says Lai Fun. It's not good to have bad blood. You might run into her some time down the road on the road. I'll cook without nuts.

Welcome, Lai Fun says, and holds Daisy/Marguerite's hands in her own. They stand in the doorway, Daisy/Marguerite still on the outside step, Lai Fun inside, and Lai Fun stares at Daisy/Marguerite's face, she can't stop staring at the lovely, familiar face. Still skinny, but healthy skinny, chipper skinny.

Welcome, Marguerite, she repeats. I know you're allergic to nuts. Does that mean sesame seeds are a no-go?

Well, says Lai Fun brightly. I can't believe it. Come in and sit down. This world is just too small. What have you been doing for the past, oh, two decades?

This joke will be told over and over again at the reunion and Lai Fun is getting her muscles primed. Hadley Constable started it at the first reunion meeting, but Lai Fun makes asking this question an art.

You look so different, says Lai Fun. You look so wonderful. So tall and strong, like an Amazon. You look so good in glasses. You haven't changed a bit. Sit down. No, you take the chesterfield, it's more comfortable. A cushy seat.

Lai Fun tries to read the designer label on the side of Daisy/Marguerite's glasses. She is sure they cost a lot of money because they are so small.

Daisy/Marguerite sinks into the couch, her long legs angling into giant knees and feet. Angélique sits opposite, in the puffy blue chair. Angélique crosses her legs right over left. Then left over right. She has already drunk three beers.

Daisy/Marguerite adjusts her spectacles at Lai Fun and says to Angélique, Has this place turned you into a tumbleweed yet?

Marguerite can't believe Angélique. She looks like Elvira, mistress of the dark. How sad that Angélique dresses in mourning for their relationship.

I'm home, says Angélique.

Would you like red or white wine, Daisy? asks Lai Fun.

I go by Marguerite now. She gives Lai Fun, a dry, soda cracker smile. What are we eating? asks Marguerite. I don't like to mix wines because it makes my stomach sour.

Lai Fun immediately feels irritated at Marguerite because exactly what is Marguerite implying?

Curried tofu and rice, says Lai Fun. A spinach and sesame seed salad.

Then I'll have white.

Which simply makes no sense to Lai Fun.

Lai Fun, says Angélique, are you going to pour the wine?

Lai Fun pours the white wine into a white wine glass, and gives the glass to Marguerite. Their fingers touch. Marguerite lifts the glass to her nose and smells the wine. Puts the glass down immediately. She turns to Angélique.

You don't like the wine? says Lai Fun.

No, says Marguerite. I know it's delicious. I'm saving it for later.

Then why aren't you drinking any? Lai Fun wants to ask. The wine is expensive. Jennifer Singh picked out the wine. Jennifer Singh may be an absentee partner and absentee parent, but she knows her wines. Seventy-two dollars a bottle. Three bottles for the evening.

Lai Fun fusses over the appetizers in the kitchen. Baked squash pouffes. Home-made baba ganouj, hummus, and melizano. She comes into the living room and sets the bowls of food down on the coffee table.

It's so strange you're sisters, says Marguerite, looking back and forth. What a coincidence. When I knew Lai Fun, she called herself Jane.

Lai Fun drops the basket of sliced baguette on the floor.

Jane? says Angélique. Really. I don't recall that.

It was a phase, says Lai Fun, coming in with the pouffes and the dips. I thought my name was too weird. We also shared a first kiss, Marguerite and I.

We did? says Marguerite. I don't remember that. You know, I think I'll try a glass of the red wine. Or beer. Do you have any beer? I could really use a beer.

Lai Fun remembers shrieking over pickled brains with Daisy in school, but now, now being with this new Daisy is like running her bare knuckles along the side of a brick house.

Angélique giggles shrilly and spills a bit of wine on her sweater.

Oops, Lai Fun says. I'll be right back with a cloth.

Luckily I'm wearing black, calls Angélique.

Freddy clutches on to Angélique's knee while he chews on a digestive biscuit and Angélique holds Freddy in front of her like a human shield. Her magic charm against selfish ex-girl-friends.

This wasn't my idea, she mouths at Marguerite.

Whaaat? mouths Marguerite.

Stefanja Dumanowski will be coming over, calls Lai Fun from the kitchen. Remember her?

Brown curly gelled hair and braces? Smart? asks Marguerite. Yeah, I remember her; she was one of those kids from the Gifted Class who sold all the drugs.

Huh? says Lai Fun. Stefanja? The Gifted Class was selling drugs?

They were all wealthy! They could afford cocaine. Marguerite crosses her legs. I remember she used to pour Bailey's over ice into her Slurpee cup.

How did Marguerite know this? Stefanja, a drug-runner for the Gifted Class? Stefanja, a sixteen-year-old alcoholic? Lai Fun pads the wet wine stain on Angélique's sweater.

The bottle opener's disappeared somehow so you'll have to stick with the white wine for now, Marguerite, says Lai Fun. So what have you been doing for twenty years? She stares at Marguerite's giant knobby knees.

My parents divorced, my father kidnapped me and my brother when I was seventeen and took us back to his family in Québec. I've been there ever since. I work for VIA Rail. I write poetry. I've published over ten books.

Oh, I'm sorry, says Lai Fun and belches. I had no idea.

Yes you did, Marguerite says. I told you all about it when it happened. I phoned you from Québec. You don't remember?

It was all so long ago. Lai Fun takes a gulp of wine. I remember we were great friends during *The Mikado*.

I liked you more than you liked me, says Marguerite.

Angélique grabs Freddy by the bum as he tries to crawl away. She pulls him back toward her.

Once you said I smelled, says Marguerite. God, kids can be horrible to each other. That's the problem with reunions. They remind you of things you don't want to remember.

Lai Fun climbs up the stairs into the bathroom. She pulls down her pants, sits on the toilet, and a hot sea gushes from her urethra. Daisy called her? After the kidnapping? Lai Fun should have run to Montréal and rescued Daisy. Daisy was the only other black girl at the school. Daisy in her brown and blue striped shirt, her hair in the ponytail scooped up on one side. Lai Fun flushes the toilet.

So are you really here for the reunion, Marguerite? asks Angélique. Or are you here simply to piss me off?

I made a big mistake. It was the pesto sauce that was the problem, not you. You know how sensitive I am around food. Well, I figured out the oil in the brand of pesto sauce we used was full of histamines and that's what was getting me down, whispers Marguerite to Angélique. Not you.

I don't want to talk to you.

I'm sorry, says Marguerite. I can't sleep because I think of that huge mistake. I'm on anti-depressants! Look at me. I've lost fifteen pounds.

So have some more pouffe.

Lai Fun on her hands and knees looking for a roll of toilet paper because of course the toilet paper has run out on the toilet paper holder. She scrabbles through the cupboard looking for another roll, but only finds an old lipstick and a dried-up bandage. She stands up and pulls up her underpants. Flushes the toilet. Straightens all the towels. Rinses out the soap dish because she hates soap scum and reunions.

Marguerite reaches for one of Angélique's hands. Angélique heaves Freddy up to her bosom and he pushes away her face with his hands.

Down! he shouts.

Do you want another cookie, Freddy? asks Angélique.

Aha! he shouts, and grabs a clump of her hair and puts it in his mouth. He meows.

I really like this town. It's not the hole it was when I went to high school here.

You're not moving back here.

Did I say I was? Jesus.

Marguerite downs her wine. I didn't come here to see you, you know. I came for the reunion. Which one's your room?

I am *not* sleeping with you, says Angélique. You said you hated high school. You said you hated it here.

Yeah, but look at me now, says Marguerite. I'm an award-winning writer. I've grown a foot and a half since high school. I feel like I'm finally in the driver's seat.

Lai Fun clumps down the stairs.

Stefanja stands in the tulip patch outside Lai Fun's house, a bottle of wine and a bouquet of chrysanthemums in her hands, and watches the three of them through Lai Fun's window. She looks at Angélique in her black outfit. Her eyes and lips heavily made up in her round, tired face, her hair piled on top of her head. She looks at Daisy. Her smooth skin. Her designer spectacles. Her small, high breasts under the tight, short-sleeved top. Seven feet tall and skinny and gorgeous. Stefanja remembers Daisy staring at her when Stefanja walked out of a toilet cubicle after she'd dropped a handful of gram bags of weed and they'd scattered all over the floor. Stefanja offered Daisy a free gram, but Daisy said, No, thank you, like Stefanja had done something wrong.

Stefanja walks back home with her wine and chrysanthemums. She would go spark up with Thor to make herself feel better, but she stopped doing that right after she became pregnant with Olivia.

Lai Fun breaks off a clump of bread, scoops it through the hummus and stuffs it into her mouth. She looks at this Daisy, now Marguerite, the wrinkles, the soft edges around her jaws, the light droop of her breasts. Has Lai Fun also changed that much? She hopes not. Her family has young genes – just look at Louve and Angélique. Lai Fun never wanted to do this reunion. Never did. And how could Daisy forget that kiss? How could she?

Angélique remembers being so fed up from all the pasta Marguerite stuffed her with, she never wanted to see another stick of cannelloni ever again. Maybe she should throw her drink in Marguerite's face. Except she's already finished her drink. Nothing but a lipstick smear on the edge of her glass. Maybe if she slept with Marguerite just one last time, Marguerite would understand that they were really over.

Marguerite hates this city, she fucking hates it, Lai Fun dull as her hors d'oeuvres, Angélique revelling in hicksville with that meowing baby full of crumbs and drool in her arms. She likes the way her legs look in her new pants. They hide her knobby knees. She hopes Angélique at least has a double bed.

CHAPTER 15

Louve dreams she sees Lai Fun slip condoms into a shopping basket. When she wakes up, Louve doesn't dare ask because Lai Fun would snap her head off. Lai Fun has said "Our neighbours Stefanja and Thor" one too many times. Louve meets Thor when she drops by too early at Lai Fun's house to give Lai Fun some placemats and Angélique a pair of socks covered in red hearts she found on super sale at Wal-Mart. As she walks up the street she sees Thor fixing Lai Fun and Jennifer's white picket fence.

And now Thor has taken to visiting Louve because Louve made the mistake of saying hello to Thor while he was straightening the white fencepost, looking into his eyes when he said, You must be Lai Fun's other sister, and she turned red as a raw beef heart, she chatted too much, like he had poured truth serum down her throat, those eyes and their giant dilated pupils, she could have sworn he was high but he was very coherent, nothing iffy about him except the pupils, and suddenly she was blabbing about running marathons at midnight and writing a novel and the sale on placemats and socks, he should get some. He and his girlish blond ringlets. The thoughtful nods at every single thing she said. He looked straight into her eyes while she talked and *didn't blink once*. Several times she just had to look away, his stare so disconcerting.

Just listen to me flapping my cake-hole, said Louve, her face still hot.

Send me some of your novel, Thor said, revealing the pink inside of his mouth. I can help you out with the difficult parts, if you want.

And he went back to his hammer and the bubbles in his level. Thor, the natural teacher.

I'll call you, said Thor, and Louve's heart stupidly palpitated. What was wrong with her?

That same night, Louve dreams of Thor and Lai Fun stirring themselves into a pudding and Louve knows.

I must clean the lies from the gutters on the roof, Louve writes, and her door buzzer buzzes and she gets up from the kitchen table full of paper and walks over to the door. She presses the button and says, Who is it? and she hears, It's Thor, and she presses the button to open the door because it is pink-mouthed Thor, her lesbian daughter's male lover, even though she never gave him her address or phone number, she never said she needed his help, he just offered it and she behaved like a fifteen-year-old girl, and his affair with her daughter makes Louve secretly happy but also unbearably sad because she knows this is no doubt a phase for Lai Fun, a lesbian mid-life crisis.

Hello, he says, out of breath. I was in the neighbourhood.

Yes? Louve smiles.

She feels she's in a high school play. She notices his eyes blinking at the dark of the apartment.

I was just dropping off a script at the post office, says Thor.

Ah, Louve says.

He stands at the door, his face sweating from climbing the stairs. Louve hears his breath, the quiet tick of the radiator.

Well, says Louve. Would you like something to drink? Would you like to come in?

I'm in. That would be great, yes. Nice. Wonderful.

Louve offers him a ginger ale because he looks so young, but he looks disappointed in a teenage boy kind of way until she jokingly offers him a glass of Fritz-Peter's home-made wine even though it's only ten o'clock in the morning.

Smells like you've been frying cow in here. Making dinner already? How's your book? he asks, glass in his hand, wine just about sloshing over the fine, Wal-Mart crystal edge. He's eager.

It's fine, Louve grunts a little as she struggles to squeeze the cork back into the bottle. She runs a glass of water for herself in the kitchen sink.

Thor drinks glass after glass after glass until the bottle is empty, but he doesn't show a single sign of getting drunk. He looks around the apartment, looks at the pictures of Lai Fun and Angélique and Freddy, says, Lai Fun, she's quite the lady, not that easy to get to know. But my wife and her, they've been taking care of the kids together.

Louve wants to ask him if he knows Lai Fun doesn't sleep with men and isn't he a little worried for his life, her youngest daughter so temperamental, but she sees it wouldn't do much good and that he's just a good-looking, not very bright, alcoholic.

He peers at the magnets on the fridge. The mini Canadian flag sticker Fritz-Peter stuck on the bottom corner of the freezer door.

So you have family in Montréal? Thor says.

I come from Ottawa.

But originally you're from Montréal.

All right.

I remember you mentioning Montréal the last time we talked. There's Mafia in Montréal, he says. Brightly.

156

There's Mafia all over.

Really. It's not like you'd find Mafia in Saskatchewan, though, Louve. Do you have a dog? I'm allergic to dog dander. I can't breathe, he coughs. Must be animal hair. Excuse me, I have to use my inhaler.

Louve takes out a cigarette from her mother-of-pearl cigarette case, and puts it between her lips. Thor darts forward with a lighter and lights her cigarette. He sits back and watches her take a drag. He inhales four puffs from his inhaler.

Can I bum a cigarette? asks Thor. I've run out.

When he bounces back to the couch, his face shows off his bouncing-boy energy and he looks at her body and hardly ever into her eyes. His personality entirely changed from that time by the fencepost. Why is he in her living room? Him. Her. Why.

So, she says.

Ah, that is the question, says Thor. To be or not to be. Ha ha ha.

Louve appreciates that he lit her cigarette without her asking, but she is irritated when he's drunk all of Fritz-Peter's wine and he quotes Shakespeare at random. Everyone who tries to be smart drags out poor, exhausted William Shakespeare. Shakespeare would have been embarrassed. Imagine. Working so hard and ending up a dead cliché.

I'm working on a novel now, did I tell you, Louve?

You mentioned a screenplay. About a Mafia heist. No, maybe that was Lai Fun who mentioned it.

Thor doesn't even blush.

Yes, my screenplay. Yes. Well, I want to take my screenplay and adapt it into a novel. And to do that I need to do a bit more research into the Mafia. If you know what I mean.

Why? Just make it up. Don't they all just make it up?

Louve sees the tumbling hair, the pink tongue, the giant vein in his neck. Smells the wine he's drunk. He is a drunk, he is a very veiny drunk.

Sure, Thor. I have to go water my garden now.

Your garden? says Thor. Where's that?

I rent a garden plot. Behind the building.

Louve gets up, puts on her sun-hat, picks up her gardening bag by the front door and slides on her shoes. Thor springs to his feet.

I'll come, he says. I would like to see your garden.

Thor hops around as Louve buries small bags of things, sprays her rose bushes, steps delicately around the herbs, her feet long and beautifully bony, he can tell, even through the white tube socks. Thor watches Louve's feet, follows her, vigorously gesticulating as he describes his novel, how right now it takes place in Montréal, how the Italian Mafia is at war with the Hell's Angels, how the fate of one Mafia family lies in the balance. How he would like to move the setting to somewhere in the United States. Chicago, perhaps, to make it more marketable.

And beautiful roses, by the way. My mother grows roses and they never get this big.

Yes, says Louve. Hybrid tea roses are very hard to grow in this climate.

I've had interest in my screenplay from a producer I worked for in Saskatchewan, Thor's voice drops used-car-salesman low.

You make a living pitching screenplays?

I make commercials, Thor says. Plumb your Way out of a Pickle with Pete the Plumber! That's me. I wrote that. But that's a commercial. Would you like to read my screenplay?

Thor pulls a wad of paper out of his ass pocket. He straightens out the fold in the centre and holds the paper out to her. Louve grabs on to the watering can with both her hands, her eyes riveting to his forearm, to the vein running down his arm, thick as an umbilical cord. *Hot* as an umbilical cord.

If you like, Louve says. Water from her hands drips onto the cover page.

158

She's in love with me, Thor thinks. Poor old biddy. I wonder if she still does it with her husband?

I planted this rose bush when Trudeau died, she says. This breed is called "Prince Charles."

Really? That's fabulous, says Thor. He takes his left hand out of his pocket and yawns.

How's your novel? he asks.

Oh, you know. Plodding away.

Found an agent?

I haven't even thought about agents. I have a third cousin who is an agent. I'll look him up when the time comes, I suppose.

She doubts the time will ever come.

You're drunk at three in the afternoon? asks Stefanja. You drove after drinking an entire bottle of wine by yourself?

Louve's lonely. She liked my company. Kept asking me about my novel.

She has grown daughters! You haven't had a contract in almost four months. Have you done any work today? Have you made any phone calls? We can't afford to break another RRSP. And you're using your inhaler. And you've been drinking. You'll be dead by the time you're forty. Baby, don't make me say it. Don't make me tell you how you're ruining your health.

Jesus Christ, quit nagging. I'll get my mother to give us money.

I don't want to keep owing your parents. It's time we grew up, baby.

Thor refuses to say what he's thinking because you can't say that kind of thing to a woman and any man who would is an asshole, but sometimes he wishes Stefanja would shut her fucking flapping cake-hole.

Did you sleep with her? asks Stefanja recklessly, ridiculously, and Thor laughs and laughs because he is drunk and the thought of him servicing poor old Louve and her disproportionately long and bony feet in their white cotton socks suddenly makes his penis very hard.

Sex with Lai Fun's mother? Sex with the mother *and* the daughter. He suddenly feels like Dustin Hoffman.

Pendulous, wrinkly breasts.

Grey pubic hair.

A saggy, bloated belly (he could see it through the cloth of her pants, poking out from under the belt cinched around her waist).

And her hips. He can't even begin to imagine her hips, but trying to imagine her hips, trying to imagine her naked ass makes his head hot. Her legs are like a twenty-year-old's. He doesn't know how a woman her age could have such legs.

No. No way. But wouldn't that be a nice gift, letting her sleep with him and his youngish, tight body. Mostly tight except for maybe his stomach, but at least he's young!

He's a little surprised at Stefanja being so angry, he thought she would think it funny, him drinking all afternoon with Lai Fun's mother in her apartment reeking of fried meat. He wonders why Stefanja isn't laughing when he can hardly stop giggling because even if the talk with Louve turned out to be a bust on the Mafia front, at least he's now got a publishing connection with her cousin the agent. He'll get the name from Lai Fun. He's tried almost every literary agent on the continent and none of them have even sniffed the bait. He was working today, making important connections. He could get in good, get the goods while he got in good. He has a good feeling about this one. A very good feeling. It goes right down to his crotch. He'll be so fucking rich and famous, he won't have to live with this dumb woman any more.

You know, I doubt the Mafia's really like this, Stefanja says when she reads his second screenplay, *Lucky Stiff*. This is just stuff the guy who wrote *The Godfather* made up. They're not noble. They're criminals doing shitty things to other people and each other. It's not glamorous. No one in their right mind would actually want to be part of the Mafia.

What do you know, says Thor, grabbing back his screenplay. Stefanja didn't read it carefully; she took forever to get around to it and then she did a half-assed job.

Excellent, says Lai Fun. This is just like *The Godfather,* only better.

She throws the screenplay on the bed. Pulls her shirt off and her dress-pants down.

You read the whole thing through that fast?

I didn't need to, I knew it would be so good.

She unhooks her maternity bra, tugs down her underpants, lies back on the bed, her stomach bulging into the air high and hard as a wedding cake. She looks at her watch.

Let's go, she says. C'mon. It's 12:34. I've got forty-five minutes.

Thanks, Lai Fun, thanks. I'm glad you like it. Do you think your mother's third cousin the agent could read it? What's your mother's cousin's name again?

Lai Fun props herself up on her elbows and stares at him.

Do you have a pen I could borrow? he asks.

She watches him pull a pad of paper from out of his coat pocket. She heaves herself up off the motel bed, pulls on her underpants, hooks up her bra, buttons her shirt, zips up her pants, sweeps on her coat, and grabs her briefcase on the way out the door.

Thor takes a puff from his inhaler. He borrows the pen on the motel desk and starts writing notes in the margins of his screenplay. His Mafia matriarch is beginning to look a lot like Lai Fun's mom. Sounds like her too. He imagines putting his tongue between Louve's big toe and second toe.

Can't talk now. Gotta write, he mumbles.

Lai Fun slams the car door closed and jacks up the air-conditioning. She wonders where she last put her vibrator.

While Jennifer, Lai Fun's un-lover wife boss, works late, works weekends, talks to Lai Fun only about the mandate review, Lai Fun fucks Thor whom she noticed from her window while he sat at his on the other side of the fence drinking coffee and typing on his computer for months. She thought the guy was surfing porn because he was puffing on his inhaler every three minutes, but then she realized his marriage to Stefanja was a joke, that men like him fuck chickens if the chickens are obvious enough, and she realized he would have to do. He is married to Stefanja, her best friend since university, but her pregnant hormones, Jennifer at work all the time and straight to sleep when she comes home, tell Lai Fun she needs skin and she needs it without delay and there he is just over the fence, sitting at his computer playing solitaire and probably surfing lesbian porn in the window behind the blinds smoking and drinking his coffee while Jennifer is busy composing Strategic Plans and Stefanja is inputting codes for fitness passes. Sometimes he mows the lawn, shovels the walk, fixes shingles, fills cracks in the steps with cement, adjust his balls with one hand while hammering with the other, and she watches these moments, watches him be a Man and do Manly things. At least he does manual labour. If she has to sleep with a man, it might as well be a Man who can fix fences and solder pipes. Lai Fun can't wait to finish being pregnant because then she will stop having anything to do with this self-involved moron, only one more month and she will be free, the pregnancy making her stupid and careless around men like Thor, men she would normally induct in her Idiot Hall of Fame. She sits on the toilet, her hands on her knees, and stares at a pool of bath-water on the floor by the tub. She prays the fetus inside her has nothing to do with Thor. Of course it doesn't, but Lai Fun is afraid her repeated contacts with Thor, his poking her cervix, may make the baby stupid or depraved. Lai Fun wonders if she should flush some tampons down the toilet back at the house and give the plumber who looks like Princess Leia a call. Would Princess Leia have sex with her? But that would be cheating, sleeping with another woman, while sleeping with Thor, well, that's not serious. It's more like, like, *masturbation*. Maybe she should talk to her psychologist. The one who looks like Al Capone.

She will name the baby Alphonsa, after Al Capone. Jennifer Singh will have to agree.

As Thor scribbles another plot twist, another witty come-back, he pictures how he will offer himself as a gift to Louve. Louve will be so grateful to him. He will use their intercourse for material in his next screenplay about a young man who has an affair with an older woman who then dies. Nothing like this has been done before. Perhaps Louve will let him take photographs of her naked. All this in preparation for his introduction to the agent, of course.

Will you read my novel, Louve? asks Thor.

I'd love to, but I'm very busy with my own, says Louve.

Would you like to trade? We could edit each other's work.

Louve cuts herself three long-stemmed roses. Thor amazed at his own selflessness.

Louve digs through her gardening bag. She is at her wit's end, losing her wits, *Thor has abducted her wits*. She scrapes the back of her hand on a spade. Lai Fun, her baby Noodle, is having an affair with a man whom Louve believes has the most bloated veins she has ever seen. Of course she can't do anything about the affair – it's none of her business. But she can't stop thinking about it. She should telephone Lai Fun but Lai Fun would hate her. She should telephone Jennifer, but she's never been close to

Jennifer; Jennifer would think Louve was trying to split her and Lai Fun up. She should talk to Fritz-Peter, but he would order her not to interfere. He would say that the state – and mothers in particular – have no place in the bedrooms of the nation. Then he would be able to tell from her face that she was thinking about another man's veins.

She pulls out an old and muddied garden and lifestyle magazine. Flips through the pages to the one she wants, then tears the page out. She won't mention the veins.

Dear Ann Landers, she writes, the page with Ann Landers' address on it beside her,

> *I hate to say it, but I believe my lesbian daughter's*
> *extramarital secret male lover is interested in*
> *having an intimate relationship with me, her*
> *mother. He has said nothing explicit, but I can*
> *tell from the way he stares at my toes that he is*
> *interested and I am dreading the day he mentions*
> *aloud his lust for me. Of course there is no way*
> *I could consider him as I am happily married*
> *and he is my daughter's lover. How should I go*
> *about handling this uncomfortable situation?*
> *My daughter doesn't know I know about her*
> *relationship. I cannot tell my husband. I have no*
> *one to talk to except you, Ann.*
>
> *Signed, Troubled in the Rose Garden*

She reads the letter over.

She rips the paper off the pad, tears it into tiny pieces, and packs them into the front pocket of her gardening bag. Compost for the flowers.

CHAPTER 16

Angélique, the daughter who looks just like Pierre Trudeau and wears long black skirts and combat boots, sits on a slippery blue bus seat. The windows coated with sprays of mud, in her head a list of baby things to buy now that she's become her sister's unofficial, grossly underpaid nanny. Not that she doesn't love Freddy, she does. She loves him so much she would drown herself in the toilet for him.

The bus stops on the bridge. She looks out the grimy window at the river, the brown-leafed trees on the riverbanks. She ran away to the west to escape bad love affairs, but they have pursued her – they have caught her. Stefanja weeping to her in the zoo about her husband, Jennifer Singh knocking on Angélique's basement door wanting to know the secret for keeping Lai Fun's love.

Lai Fun is a garden maze, said Angélique. And no one, not even Lai Fun, has a map.

But I'm only doing all this for her, said Jennifer. I work so hard. Why does she think me working means I don't love her? She hates it when I'm gone, but it seems like she hates me even more when I'm home.

Have you gone to a marriage counsellor?

No couple I know who goes to marriage counselling ever survives. Our friends Maddie and Helen went to marriage counselling and they broke up after a twenty-three year relationship. Counselling is instant bad luck.

Have you talked to her? Bought her a bag of her favourite nuts?

I buy her nuts. I buy her earrings. I buy her clothes. I married her when she wanted me too. I should have said no. I forgot that fifty percent of marriages end in divorce. That's what I should have told her. We got married. Now we're doomed.

In despair and depression, Jennifer sinks to the floor next to the furnace.

Can I boil you some pasta? asks Angélique.

In her black clothes, Angélique is a black hole attracting love misery. Maybe she should start wearing red.

Angélique makes room on her bus seat for the Suit with the moustache to sit beside her even though he must have seen her bag on the seat. Once upon a time, she was a Suit, she had several suits, she dated Suits, she cared about which suit and which Suit. She entertains the idea of asking the Suit beside her for a job as a joke, except the fact that he's taking the bus when most Suits in this city drive to work makes her wonder if maybe he's a fake Suit after all. His coat is expensive. She peeks at his shoes – highly polished, very nice. Maybe he's slumming.

A noisy crew of school kids with baseball caps on backward and still-wet hair and naked belly-buttons push the Suit against Angélique. Piss her off. Their backpacks remind her of her own little bag when she was little – back in the old country – full of fossilized oranges because Louve always gave Angélique oranges with her lunch and Angélique hated oranges so much she'd let them turn into orange baseballs. She also let the oranges turn into baseballs when she lived in Montréal back when she had her own fridge. Seems like Angélique hasn't had her own fridge for ages now. She had a great fridge in Montréal, one of those old 1950s ones that they outlawed because little kids kept locking themselves into them and suffocating to death and then the Suit wrecks her walk down memory lane by putting his stupid Suit hand on her ass like it's an accident or something and she's so fucking furious she wrenches his hand out from where it's been working its way to her asshole and she drives up his hand into the air and says out loud so that all the other fake Suits and the teenage kids and their belly-buttons can hear: WHOSE HAND IS THIS? THIS IS NOT MY HAND, BUT IT WAS GRABBING MY ASS.

And so some stupid jerk Suit ruins her morning, ruins her week, ruins her month and probably the rest of her life. Not that it wasn't ruined anyway with all the bad love affairs and no job and no ideas for a job in sight, and Freddy cereal all over the front of her skirt. She expects maybe applause after her announcement, but instead at the next bus stop, long before downtown where all these Suits live and all these kids go to school, everyone in the bus spills down the bus steps out the bus doors, one after the other falling out into the street. She is the only one left on the bus because even the driver has left supposedly to grab a coffee even though the bus is five minutes late. Her ass gets grabbed, but she's the loopy one.

The world should go fuck itself. But of course it'll fuck her over first. She glares out the window. Glares at the stone griffins perched on Crooks' Drugstore.

Marguerite was boiling another pot of pasta when Angélique said she was going to move west.

But why? asked Marguerite. You love Montréal. What's out west that you can't get here?

My family. You not there.

But when I dumped you I didn't mean for you to leave town, said Marguerite. Sexually we're perfectly compatible. We're just not meant for a domestic partnership.

I don't want us to be sex-puppets, said Angélique miserably, pasta steam making her forehead hot and sticky.

They fell into bed.

Marguerite will think of drowning herself in one of the saucepans of pasta cream sauce once Angélique leaves. Marguerite has lost her muse, but for Angélique, being a muse is *boring*. Marguerite will write her best book of poetry when Angélique leaves and win the continent's top poetry prize.

Maybe it was the dumping. Maybe it was the morning Angélique allowed herself to take off work or else her mind would come clattering out of her pockets like her house keys. She defended vindictive neighbours, sexual harassers, corrupt organizations for so long. Maybe she was too weak to be a lawyer. Maybe it was good they laid her off.

She feels like crap even after she's gone to the mall and picked up Freddy's prescription and other Freddy odds and ends. Back on the bus, it's the much calmer raisin set with their stiff white hair-do's and plastic rain bonnets going wherever it is they go. A seniors' community centre? The central library? Bingo? The bar? Some have curlers on under their hair-nets; Angélique thinks these ones are the cutest. Nothing more comforting than a woman in her curlers on the bus. Angélique swears she will do this too one day, the day she becomes a grown-up and stops looking to Freddy for advice and protection.

CHAPTER 17

Strawberries in season, dollar forty-nine a pint. Three whole chickens, five dollars a pound. Underwear, fifteen pairs for fifteen dollars, so Louve buys fifteen – seven for herself, and eight for Lai Fun, who complains about her maternity bum. Angélique needs something too – bad to give presents to one daughter and not the other, no matter how old they are. Navel oranges, dollar seventy a pound, so Louve buys four big, sweet ones. Angélique's favourite snack since she was a child. A package of beef sausage.

Thor leans over the edge of the shopping cart and watches Louve in her long overall dress, her feet in white socks and sandals, shop. She told him he could come only if when he talked he didn't use the letter "i."

A word game, he says. I should be good at that.

You blew it already, Louve says and laughs, then frowns at the price of asparagus. Who can actually afford asparagus? Who would agree to afford asparagus?

Thor watches the sway of Louve under her dress.

The other day Fritz-Peter came home wearing full-price cowboy boots he'd charged to his Visa. She nearly had a fit; too bad he looked *very* sharp in all that stitched leather. But then he got blisters because he wore the wrong socks and lurched around in the high heels so long he threw out his back for a whole afternoon.

I've been thinking, Thor starts. She shushes him.

This is silly –

Six "i"s I heard, says Louve.

The least she could do is talk instead of mutter to herself over bins of bargain underwear and asparagus. If he's not allowed to talk, then why doesn't she talk? What's the point of wasting his day here? What is she trying to find when she squeezes the oranges like that? A pearl?

Listen, he says.

One "i."

But this is no longer funny, in fact it was never funny and from the beginning he didn't understand the point. He suddenly stands up straight and pushes the grocery cart away from him.

Fuck this, Louve.

I thought you were going to help me carry groceries on the bus? I'm not going to stop eating because you're feeling pouty.

I –

Shush!

I know –

What?

I have a plan.

She picks up a papaya and rolls it impatiently in her hands before dropping it back with the others.

I think we should exchange novels, Louve. You look at mine. I'll look at yours.

But I don't want to. You've been writing much longer. I would be embarrassed.

I could help you, he says.

No, Thor. No.

Fine, he says, and he waddles off in his emperor penguin-like way and she is trapped with a shopping cart full of food and no way to get it home.

Thor! she calls. All right! Let's do it.

He pirouettes around and comes towards her with his hands and face open.

We'll learn so much from each other. I know it.

Of course, she says.

Thor knows her novel will be terrible: beginning writers don't know how to keep autobiography out of anything. She'll have written about dusting or vacuuming and raising children – chick lit shit – but maybe she will mention her Mafia family, the creepy people she holds company with, even this far away from Montréal. Maybe he'll take her ideas and turn them into great literature. The least he'll get is access to an agent.

And when he reads Louve's novel, he wants to kill himself and masturbate and scream all at once. Because the book makes him sick. Louve doesn't have the right. She's an old biddy with a first draft that makes him feel like a number-one fuck-up. How could a *housewife* like Louve know all these things? She can't write for shit, but her knowledge, her *experience*, make him look like hacked meat.

What're you reading? says Stefanja.

I'm *working*, he says, sweat dripping from his forehead onto the paper. He needs a puff.

Oh. Well. I'm going for a run. I'll bring in Olivia. She needs to be changed.

I'm in the middle of making *art*, I don't have *time* to change a shitty *diaper*. When will you understand that? *Art has no time for diapers.*

Who do you think you are? Jackson Fucking Pollock? I've been – sup-sup-supporting you – for years – cleaning up after you – taking care of your daugh-daugh-daughter – for years – so you can – so you can – so you can –

Stefanja stops because she has accidentally pushed all the air from her lungs.

In the very back of his brain, Thor supposes he deserves it when he feels and hears and smells the diaper slap the back of his neck. He supposes he deserves it, but damn it, he calls his mother anyway.

Screw this life.

He is moving to L.A.

CHAPTER 18

Lai Fun dreams of noodles. She dreams of Thor placing a bowl of noodles in front of her on one of her mother's Wal-Mart placemats and Lai Fun is almost delirious when she wakes up because finally she has dreamed of something that hasn't already happened and she hasn't dreamed of griffins; Thor has never, ever, served her noodles, those placemats are in a box in the basement ready for the Sally Ann, and not a single griffin feather or hair entered the scene, her imagination has kicked in again. She has an imagination! She wonders what the dream means. She has felt ambivalent for a long time about having the nickname Noodle as a thirty-eight-year-old woman. Maybe she should just keep the nickname and forget about it. That's what the dream means. Of course. The baby punches and kicks hello in her belly. She clucks quietly and pats its head or its bum. She gets up to go check on Freddy and to relish the memory of her dream. She hunts in the dark for her glasses, which have gone missing from the bedside table, of course. How she loves having her imagination back.

CHAPTER 19

Thursday, Louve assembles a basket of things she can mend at work: holey socks, a duffle bag, one of Fritz-Peter's Hawaiian shirts. Maybe she will make him a bag to hold his crocheting for his birthday.

The front door opens, and she remembers she didn't lock it, stupid stupid.

Who's that? she calls, socks and shirts in her hand. Who's there? Fritz-Peter? Are you home already?

It's me, she hears.

Who's me? Is that you? Thor?

Probably that twit the primatologist who lives downstairs must have let him in the building and she should have locked her front door, she always locks the front door, but she heard an ambulance this morning and rushed into the hallway to look out the big window to make sure the ambulance wasn't going in the direction of Lai Fun's house. Very stupid. Now she can't even pretend not to be at home. She leaves the bedroom and Thor is in the front hall with a bottle of sparkling wine and a bouquet of flowers as though flowers can buy hearts and Louve suddenly feels very sorry for his wife and for Lai Fun. He

puts the flowers and wine on the kitchen counter, then he un-
zips his pants and strips down to his underwear in one elegant,
ostrich-like motion.

Thor! she says shrilly. Put those pants back on!

Thor behaves brazenly and sexily. She is a married woman,
she is older than the hills. Maybe when she was twenty and
didn't know any better, a barely dressed man, dumb but beautiful and full of veins, would have turned her on, but right now
she might regurgitate her soy and oatmeal. Louve suddenly
gets very tired of being Thor's perpetual audience and when
he asks her to please call his penis Samuel Beckett, she has had
enough. Now he is dragging out poor Beckett when Beckett of
all people deserves some peace.

You hid your book from me, he says, and waggles his index
finger in her face. Because you knew how I was writing about
almost exactly the same thing. You knew it would make me
look like an idiot when you read mine. You were teasing me,
Louve.

Thor, put your trousers on or I'll call Ann Landers.

Ann Landers?

Lai Fun. Not Ann Landers, Lai Fun, I mean.

Louve, murmurs Thor, I want to lie down with you. I want
to make love to you.

My book's not that good, Thor.

No, it's not. Did you read mine?

Well – I – have been doing a lot of night shifts and I –

It's all right. It's terrible. Lie down with me, Louve. You
have to. Because I know what you are.

What am I, Thor?

You're not like other people, he says, stupid and erect and
drunk. And I love your legs.

Louve crumples the shirt in her hand into a ball. He's noticed her legs?

I've seen into your *soul*, Louve, I've seen into your heart and I want to get inside you. Where do you really come from, Louve? You're not from here.

I *am* from here, Thor. It says so in my citizenship papers.

You're a daughter of night and the mother of fate. Do you really have two sisters you never speak to? Can they really change shape at will? Don't you ever want to go back home, Louve?

She bares her teeth. I am home, she says. I was *invited*.

Red maple leaves in autumn, Trudeau in his white cowboy hat, Trudeau saying the state has no business in the bedrooms of the nation, the day she passed her citizenship exam, the day her all-Canadian, perfectly bicultural, bilingual baby was born, she tries to forget about Trudeau's stupid NEP idea and him being so mean to those poor farmers about their wheat, but the one thing she can't bear, no matter how long she lives, how many times she hears it, is people asking her where she's *really* from. As though she could not possibly come from this country and belong to this soil. This she cannot bear.

Louve, Thor whispers. Tell me about back home. They say good artists borrow, but great artists steal. *Let me steal, Louve.*

Daisy in her hotel room writing furiously in her notes about the kind of love one can only make with an ex-lover. Her stomach sour from bad white wine.

Angélique on the big blue bus pulling away from the griffins and realizing she's never noticed them on that particular drugstore before.

Lai Fun napping, dreaming of stirring orange juice with a tennis racquet and, in her arms, Freddy sucking his toe in his sleep.

Fetus playing yet another game of solitaire.

The roses in Louve's garden, gently rising out of the earth, as though with someone's breath.

A chinook wind roiling on the horizon.

Louve stares at Thor, stares at the capillaries in his nose, the veins in his forehead; she hears the pump of his aorta, his pulmonary arteries, the descent of his blood through the celiac, gastric, femoral arteries, the rush of the blood from his heart to his brain to his guts. The perfect blue of the veins in his arms, the distended jugular on the side of his throat, she could never resist a perfect vein, the sound of venous music, she even hears a light, unresolved venous hum around his throat that makes her cock her ears, and she darts her teeth forward to snap and tear off the waggling finger because she could never stand waggling fingers, ever since she was a girl. The finger drops from her mouth, rolls and bumps across the floor. She jumps, spread-eagled, onto Thor's neck as he stares stupidly at where his finger used to be and even as she is doing it she feels bad about jumping at his neck, she does, unable to resist the giant, beautiful vein, her years away from the hospital make her ravenous for a decent vein, but she is no animal, what separates her from animals is her self-control. Or maybe she is an animal, she's forgotten after so many years of tofu and chickpeas and alfalfa sprouts, the taste of live flesh such a *relief*.

Thor pushes her off and stumbles away so she hooks the tendons on the backs of his knees with her fingernails and he falls forward, shouts in pain first from the shock of the teeth, then from the shooting in his knees as he falls to the kitchen

177

linoleum, then he is silent because Louve has her teeth lodged in his very thick neck, that jugular vein ambrosia and essence of roses and frying meat and his voice has fluttered away from his throat along with his startled spirit.

This is not how Thor would have chosen to die. If anyone had offered him various choices, he would have laughed because he, Thor, was never going to die, but if he had to choose, why, a gun, of course. Fast and simple and dramatic for the survivors, not stupid like this, not humiliating like this. Chewed and swallowed by a monstrous old *housewife*. A housewife wearing *tube socks*.

The first rushes of Thor in her mouth all to herself.

The metaphor roars and violently shakes its head like there's a horsefly stuck in its ear, and she wonders, Does her eating Thor make her an adulteress? Worse still, what about all the blood? And after years of vegetarianism, she wonders if all this sudden red meat protein is good for her. A lot of blood straight up gives her gas, but she has to suck all his blood because otherwise there will be too much mess and evidence and stickiness and explanation. Even with her sucking the blood as fast as she is, a stream meanders its way to the very expensive Persian carpet in the living room and if the carpet gets stained she will weep because she really loves that carpet. That carpet one of the few things left from the boom days.

And the only choice left is eating him in order to dispose of the body – this is what she had to do before she became a nurse and could dispose of the bodies without too much problem at the morgue or in pieces in the incinerator. Before she and Fritz-Peter turned over new leaves and became vegetarians so they could set an example for Lai Fun. They were getting too old to deal with hiding bodies and making up stories and moving to yet another shitty town in the boonies; a new baby made things complicated and they would not make the same mistakes with Lai Fun that they made with Angélique when she was growing up. They wanted to live in one place for a long time. Put down roots deep into the earth and live normal, boring suburban lives forever.

But Louve is not a nurse anymore; she has no easy access to a hospital. And Thor is no drifter or stranger in town; people will miss him. And what about all the new forensic technology, the carpet and clothing fibres, microscopic hair fragments, saliva and cells from the walls of her mouth? She cannot leave him here or dump him in some cobble-stoned side street, drag him about the hallways and up and down elevators; she will have to eat him to dispose of the body, eat him all and she will have to do it quickly before the police arrive. Before Fritz-Peter finds out. She will never be able to hide it from Fritz-Peter.

Too much meat overall is a big problem, but also all the fat and bone and tendons – god! – so much gristle will give her horrible runs and heartburn for days. Years ago, when she had a stronger metabolism, her stomach could handle bones, hair, nails, teeth, but all the cartilage is getting hard on her teeth – now capped because she was careless when she was younger. She sucks and sucks at his neck until most of the blood is gone. She pulls the roll of paper towel from its holder and runs to the stream and blots up the spill, fast. As she wipes, she sucks the soggy paper towel, sucks it and stares at Thor who invited her into the world of adultery, stares at the carpet from the old days during the oil boom, stares at the wall, at her faint shadow on the wall. Too many shadows on the wall.

The phone rings. Fritz-Peter.

Get home now, says Louve into the receiver.

I can't leave until the end of my shift. Guess who held me up today? Boris. Remember Boris Ignatieff? We've been talking about the old days and I've invited him over for dinner tonight. I'll cook. We can have a nice eggplant shepherd's pie. Do I need to pick up some eggplant on the way home?

I've killed Lai Fun's lover.

Lai Fun's lover? The commercial man? You shouldn't interfere with her life. She hates that.

I couldn't help it.

What have you done with the body?

Fritzy! Let's have a dinner party.

You mean *keep* the body? *We're not like that anymore.*

Fritz-Peter hates italics. He never speaks in italics except in extreme situations.

Yes! A dinner party. We haven't eaten meat in almost thirty years.

There's no one to invite any more. Everyone left when they lost their jobs. Look, we can find some other way.

You found Boris, you can find the others.

What about Lai Fun? Are you going to tell her you killed her lover and you'd like her to help eat him?

He was trying to seduce me. There's no time, Fritz-Peter. I don't know if anyone is expecting him, or knows that he came here. What if the police or his mother or someone come looking?

I'll bring home a video. We can watch it with Boris. Boris lost his job. Lai Fun's lover tried to seduce you? With what?

Louve hangs up. Louve is getting too old for having to dispose of bodies. Much, much easier when she worked at the hospital and could just take the bits and pieces as she needed when the craving was too bad, when she could suffer the bloating and the diarrhea. Which she hasn't done since she was forced to retire ten years ago. But she was not born to fast and neither was Fritz-Peter. And it doesn't help that she sucked back three bottles of wine, ten sucks at the asthma inhaler, and two breakfast marijuana joints along with all that blood.

Louve gets out the Mr Clean.

CHAPTER 20

Thor's mother Asta wants out of her marriage; Thor is no longer into his. His mother wants him to be famous; Thor wants fame. There is no other option. Stefanja can take care of herself. He will miss Olivia, but knows when Olivia is older and past the messy toddler stage she will understand why her father had to do this and she will benefit from being connected to someone rich and famous – he will come back for Olivia once he's settled himself down. Asta wanted to take Olivia along without telling Stefanja, but Thor knew that Stefanja would probably come after them with an axe.

Dear Stefanja, he writes,

> *I want to write to you about truth and love and the*
> *pursuit and creation of beauty in its many forms.*
> *Love is Plasticine, it doesn't disappear, it transfers*
> *and changes shape. When we first married you*
> *agreed how important it was for me to follow my*
> *bliss so that's what I'm doing. You've found your*
> *bliss in our child. A thing has happened that makes*
> *me realize that my bliss is just around the corner.*

It is, finally, my turn to follow through on my
promise to you, but seeking out my own bliss.

You know my email address, my lovely love, write
me there in case of emergency. I won't be able to
answer you right away because I don't know where
I'll be. But I will be thinking of you and Livy.
Don't be cross with me.

Your husband, Thor

He leaves the letter on her pillow. Arranges it on the smooth curve. He changes his mind and moves the letter to the coffee table where she might see it sooner, then to the dining room table because that's more obvious and the first thing you see when you walk in the door; on the other hand, the first thing she normally does is go straight to the kitchen so he props it in front of the microwave. He sticks it with a magnet to the fridge. Ultimately it looks much better, makes the best statement, taped to the bathroom mirror where Stefanja can look at herself and see what a beautiful woman she is.

He sets out his luggage on the front porch and locks the door behind him. Then he slides the letter into the mail slot in the front door.

First, he will stow his luggage in a locker at the airport, then he will go to Louve; then he will meet his mother at the airport and they will fly away to Los Angeles with the tickets his mother bought. He will rewrite his manuscript using Louve's manuscript as his content basis. He will convert his novel into a screenplay that he will also sell. He will be famous. His mother will be his agent. A perfect plan.

Thor's mother Asta waits for Thor in "Up and Away," the

lounge at the airport. She sips her cool and delicious white wine spritzer, gazes at the television. Soon she will have another white wine spritzer, then another, then a fourth, then a glass of plain white wine, then a whiskey with ice, then whiskey straight. Then she will remember to take her Prozac.

She will board the plane, the one unused ticket to Los Angeles still in her purse, she and the plane long gone and Thor not on it. She puts her purse in the seat he should have been in. She will put on her sleep mask, put in her earplugs, and lie in her seat and not sleep, just ride the spin of the plane. She didn't leave her husband a carefully thought-out letter. She just left. The phone in her Los Angeles hotel room will ring, but she won't answer. She doesn't care if it's Thor because once again he's let her down, she knew he wouldn't come through, her son the coward, the disappointment, what did she do to have such a son, she should have had other children – no – she shouldn't have had any children at all, she never wanted children, it was her husband, King Moron, who wanted children. Wanted a beautiful, blond, baby boy. Wanted a whole football team of them.

She will worry about money later. For now, she will go read a magazine and have an icy margarita by the pool.

Already Olivia misses her father and fusses. There is no question of Stefanja Dumanowski going to the reunion the day after her husband has left her. Impossible even though she's committed herself to entertaining everyone's children during the softball game. A mistake, since Olivia is really the only child Stefanja likes. And Freddy, but only when he's with Angélique. Although Freddy sometimes behaves more like a baby animal than a baby human. She must work on self-care first. She plops Olivia in front of the TV in the exercise room, then jumps onto the exercise bike and pedals as though she is going somewhere.

Later, she will eat a family-sized box of chocolate-dipped granola bars. Her mouth full of granola and chocolate chips, she calls her hairdresser even though it's 12:40 at night. Tomorrow she will get her hair dyed Peacock Blue.

At 12:42, she dials Angélique's number. She chats about the TV show she watched last night, *Hollywood Law*, and asks if any of the show could really happen in real life. Like the woman who murders her husband, but then gets acquitted because he provoked her with his bad cooking.

Probably, answers Angélique.

CHAPTER 21

They will have a huge dinner once they get the various cuts of meat and parts sorted out. Lai Fun and Jennifer Singh, Baby Freddy who's never been to a dinner party, but it's about time he tried something other than baby soy products. Boris Ignatieff from Fritz-Peter's time at Texaco, Dr Stoker from the hospital cigarette and book club days, Ed Cloutier from the geological institute, a possible girlfriend for Boris, a possible boyfriend for Ed, Stoker's fourth wife, the retired professional downhill skier, Nancy. Anyone else they can find. Fritz-Peter will have to write a speech. Start with a spicy rump salad. Arden, a nurse from the hospital, has offered to make a honey-garlic sauce. Platters of seasoned meat, braised shanks, and bowls and bowls of Fritz-Peter's stupendous sauerkraut, skewers, many skewers, they can't wait for the skewers of skin like crackling. Fritz-Peter's brain fritters and sherried sweetbread, Louve's deep-fried fingers and toes in black bean sauce, prairie oysters (supplemented with some of the beef kind), braised shanks, ear and okra soup, tripe something or other, barbecued ribs, marinated flanks stuffed with oyster and giblet stuffing.

Heaps of fresh sourdough bread and bowls of butter. Fried

bananas. Some light flambé fruit for dessert. Raspberries? Cherries? Little glasses of bitters to settle everyone's stomachs. And a light custardy pudding. Fritz-Peter would rather have crème caramel.

You have to make it then, says Louve, her hands sorting through cracked pepper, dry mustard, shallots, lemons. Lemons an underrated fruit.

(The joint chequing account so empty it whistles. Louve has finally cashed the cheque Lai Fun hid in the bread box.)

I don't have time to make all those rinky-dink things, she says. Don't pout! Just make it yourself.

Louve and Stoker and Fritz-Peter and Boris and Ed will cook and cook and eat and eat just like the old days. They will get up and down in the night with gas and the shits because the meal will be too rich, but it will be worth it, such a wonderful meal. Leftovers for days.

Louve takes the bus from work in the direction of home, in the direction of the pink clouds, the bubbling, chinooking prairie sky. When she gets off the bus, she swings her purse and sings out loud she is so happy, she sings so everyone can hear her, the people on the street, the leaves falling from the trees, the old friends from the boom days before everything fell apart; her teeth exposed to the fresh, bright wind, her jaw cradling her voice and her breath.

Canada, the land of liberation. Like singing out loud in the street, like walking for the first time in the sunlight. Like learning to love garlic, crave the blood inside eggplants, like the first cup of Nabob in the morning, like the first bud on a rosebush you planted yourself. All part of being Canadian.

LOUVE'S DEEP-FRIED FINGERS IN BLACK BEAN SAUCE
(can also be done with toes although the skin will be chewier)

500 g	fingers
2.5 L	canola oil for deep frying
2.5 L	water
28 g	fresh ginger
3	pieces star anise
57 g	Chinese parsley roots
57 g	honey or maltose syrup

Marinade:

30 mL	oyster sauce
15 mL	sugar
30 mL	soy sauce
15 mL	sake or white wine
28 g	chilli pepper, chopped
2	cloves garlic, minced
2 mL	white pepper
15 mL	black bean sauce
2 mL	sesame seed oil

Rinse fingers in cold water very well. Chop off nails if long.
Mix fingers with maltose or honey syrup and fry until golden
brown, about 7 minutes. Remove and drain.

Boil water and add ginger, star anise, and parsley roots. Add
fingers. Bring to boil again, then reduce heat and simmer 90
minutes. Drain.

Combine marinade ingredients. Marinate fingers 24 hours.
Before serving, steam fingers and let sit for 15 minutes.
Serves 6.

1	brain (chopped)
175 mL	vinegar
500 mL	bread crumbs (medium to fine)
2	eggs
3	cloves garlic
	salt, pepper to taste

(That's a cop-out, says Louve. Add some basil. Some oregano. Some dried chili or cayenne pepper and some lemon. Things like that.)

1 mL	dry mustard
500 mL	canola oil for deep-frying

Bring brain pieces to boil in vinegar-water. Turn down heat to low. Simmer for fifteen minutes. Drain pieces and pull membrane off. Chop up pieces and transfer to a large bowl. Cool. Brain should be at crumbling consistency. Add bread crumbs, seasoning, and eggs to give the fritters cohesion. Deep fry in hot oil until golden brown, drain on paper towels to get rid of the excess oil. Serve immediately.

PART IV

---◆---

THE REUNION:
OCTOBER 2005

CHAPTER 22

Tonight: Cocktails, Dinner & Dance at the community hall on the former General Hospital site. "Wow Have You Changed" night, Lai Fun's night, the best night of all. She'll show Hadley Constable and Wendell Morgan and Lloyd and Maureen Weaselhead. Easy to predict the students who will come; Lai Fun ticks them off one by one on her fingers and toes and then back to her fingers.

Someone has fingered the words WASH ME into the dust on the side of Lai Fun's car, but she has no time to wipe it off because she needs big wire curlers from the drug store. Freddy unwound the springs in all the ones she had.

She wonders if any of them speak French any more. If twelve years of French immersion have completely worn off. She has been to France once, several times to Québec when her sister lived there, and every time she's stumbled through the language just fine, mixed up her vous and tus, but food tastes better in French. "Soupe de Fraises" so much more romantic than Strawberry Soup. Food, normally the bane of her existence because it takes so much time away from her busy day, suddenly becomes a work of art and language and sensuality. Beurre d'arachides et confiture.

WASH ME S'IL VOUS PLAIT her car reads when she leaves the drugstore with a bag full of jumbo wire curlers, a can of Comet cleanser, and a carob health-bar. She grinds the gears furiously because she will ignore the graffiti, she has no time for merde now. She starts to back out, then realizes it wasn't Comet she needed, it was talcum powder for under her breasts and in her armpits. She slams the door and runs back into the drugstore. Exits with a package of Chiclets and steel wool for the dirty pots even though she doesn't like steel wool for dirty pots – this is Jennifer Singh's preference, though she never does dirty pots. A carob cherry bar that's already out of the package and part-way to its sticky, runny end in her mouth when she sees above the WASH ME: J'AI BESOIN D'UNE DOUCHE.

She swipes at the words with her sticky thumb and wrist. A shower?

Suddenly her bag rips itself open and the box of steel wool, a box of condoms, the package of Chiclets bounce to the ground.

She guns the engine, pulls the strap over her belly and between her monstrous breasts and drives home. She parks the car in front of her house. On the passenger side door someone's traced in their best finger-sized font: LEZ FUN.

She swipes at the LEZ FUN with the side of her hand. Dust smears down the front of her black smock, on her sleeve. The barrette holding one of her pigtails together sproings open. Her car keys are ripped from her hand and land in the gutter and she has to grunt and contort like a hippo to get the keys back, her ass in the air for the entire neighbourhood to see. She would kick the car but she is wearing her open-toed platform mules, the only shoes that still fit her swollen but freshly manicured feet. She will wash her hair, put in the rollers, and make herself gorgeous. She will *glow*. PAKI FOON on the trunk, but she doesn't see it because she's gathered up the bags and run into the house to her sister Angélique and Freddy. "Paki" a reminder of her elementary and high school days when everyone was called Paki no matter what.

Communications from the dead.

Lai Fun wears black leather maternity pants, cost her a bloody fortune, and a silver halter top that shows her bare back and her boobs. For once she has boobs, why not show them off? Too bad about the eight-month pregnant belly to go with them. Her black mules, of course, and a little silver toe-ring to match her silver toenails.

You look like a pregnant hooker, says Angélique, Freddy twisting in her arms. You look like a human disco-ball.

So? says Lai Fun, smoothing lipstick on her lips. Life is not a dress rehearsal.

What does that mean? You say that, and I don't know what you mean. I'd rather chew my own arm off –

You would not! Don't say that!

– and eat the fingers one by one than go to a stupid reunion with a bunch of people I haven't thought about in a hundred years!

And you wonder why you're so miserable.

Cuz seeing Marguerite made *you* jump for joy.

Eee Eee Eee! shouts Freddy. He flutters his arms like a bird.

Could you change him for me? asks Lai Fun, her left eyelid glittering like an emerald beetle-wing. I don't want to get my outfit dirty.

That's what you hardly pay me for, grumbles Angélique. That and unplugging condoms from the toilet.

Fuck off!

So pathetic. Screwing a man while your wife's busy at work. What kind of lesbian are you?

I – I – I – I – don't. Have sex in this house!

Not a very convincing one, apparently. Well, *someone* flushed those condoms down the toilet. Wasn't me, needless to say, and if it wasn't you then someone found them, brought them here, and wants to rat you out. You better watch out.

The telephone rings.

Communications from the dead.

Lai Fun zips off in her car and after Freddy finishes waving at Lai Fun's cloud of exhaust, he sits in front of Angélique with his legs in that pretzel shape only little children can do and listens to her play her ukulele. Stefanja's daughter Olivia watches Freddy, watches Angélique, watches the strings of the ukulele, puts her left hand in her mouth and gnaws.

Plink! says the ukulele.

Fudge! says Angélique.

She crosses her legs and her red heart-covered socks flash for a moment from under her long black skirt. She readjusts her fingers, hunkers down around the ukulele, and plucks three notes.

Plink plink plonk! says the ukulele.

Fuuuudge! My dog has fleas! Fuddle! Angélique pretends to hammer the ukulele into the floor.

Freddy giggles out of control. Olivia takes her hand out of her mouth and begins to eat the corner of the music book.

Liona Boyd she ain't, Freddy thinks. José Feliciano she will never be. She can't even manage Tiny Tim. She is a Maria von Trapp without a mission and a Mary Poppins without the umbrella.

Freddy wiggles his legs in a ukulele dance.

CHAPTER 23

"Let the Eastern Bastards Freeze in the Dark," "This Car Doesn't Brake for Liberals," "I'd Rather Push This Thing a Mile Than Buy Gas from Petrocan." The art of the bumper-sticker. It was always lovely when an anti-Petrocan *did* push her car into Fritz-Peter's gas station and ask for help, which Fritz-Peter did with a little half-smile and extreme efficiency – not only filling up the tank and checking the oil and windshield-washer fluid levels, but also wetly sweeping the windshield and hooting his "Have a nice day" even though he was technically an Eastern Bastard and he worked at a Petro-Canada gas station. Pierre Elliott Trudeau Rips Off Canada. The battle of the words. Of the letters. The idea that Trudeau could somehow be insulted out of office. Living in the west it was hard to love Trudeau completely.

But that was back in the day and those bumper-stickers were faded and peeling by the time he started working at the gas station. The bumper-stickers are not nearly so exciting any more; duelling Jesus and Darwin fish are the best these days. Fritz-Peter sits on his stool next to the rack of gum and potato chips and waits for the next car; he scrapes car grease out from under his fingernails, combs his beard and moustache, picks his teeth with the antique silver toothpick he carries on a chain around his neck. The other gas station attendant – Sid – once called him a big fairy and Fritz-Peter asked Sid if he was insecure about his sexuality.

Since when is personal grooming equated with homosexuality, Sid? asked Fritz-Peter. Are you worried because you find yourself attracted to me? That's all right. I'm married, but that's all right. I am aware of my qualities as an attractive man. My two daughters are lesbians, and let me tell you, they're not the cleanest girls, although they try their best. I understand same-sex attraction.

Since Fritz-Peter moved west, personal grooming and care for his appearance made him into a homosexual. Sid won't take this any further, though.

But what does Fritz-Peter care? Gasoline fumes have burnt the hairs out of his nose. Once upon a time he was a geologist in a large, airy office, surrounded by rock samples and maps and the antique porcelain cups he drank his coffee from. He thought he was an oilman. Now he is *truly* an oilman, oil on his hands, smeared on his face, his front, leaked on his shoes, and staining his trousers.

And when the man in the George W. Bush mask holds the gun up to Fritz-Peter's face and shouts, Empty the till! Fritz-Peter doesn't take it personally because those bullets he can see down the muzzle of the gun have nothing to do with him, they have to do with the sagging economy; it would take more than a few store-bought bullets to defeat Fritz-Peter's spirit and as long as the bullets aren't made of silver, as long as they aren't made of wood and aimed directly into his heart, well, who gives a toot?

Boris! exclaims Fritz-Peter, looking at the eyes in the mask: one brown, the other green.

What? Just empty the till!

Boris Ignatieff, says Fritz-Peter. It's me. It's Fritz-Peter Kugelheim!

And Boris lowers the gun a fraction of a centimetre because the delicate taste of some very fine cognac Fritz-Peter once served him blossoms in his mouth, and he bursts into tears.

Boris, Boris, take off your mask, use a Kleenex. What the hell are you doing?

Fritz-Peter puts his arm around Boris's shoulder as Boris heaves with sobs, his life has come to this.

They both lost their high-flying jobs. Cars ding waiting for a fill-up, an oil-check, scrape the bugs off the windshield please, but Fritz-Peter hardly blinks as the cars screech away because he and Boris talk about the old days when they had tons of money and the economy was booming and it seemed as though everyone could afford steak and lobster.

I have stumbled in my duties as breadwinner, sighs Fritz-Peter. Maybe I wasn't such a great geologist. But you know, we manage. And in this job, Boris, you would not believe how many people I meet!

Things have to get better, says Boris, honking his nose into a paper towel. I know they will. It's just the gaps between the good times. I'm just short, you know. The severance package I got when they laid me off seemed so good twenty years ago, but inflation –

Of course things will get better, says Fritz-Peter, pouring water into the coffee machine. He clicks the ON button and the machine gurgles awake.

There's consulting, says Fritz-Peter. There's Libya. Everyone went to Libya, but Louve and I love Canada. We wanted to stay here.

Fritz-Peter looks at Boris's face, a little craggier, a little greyer, and Boris sees Fritz-Peter's face, fuller, balder. This is the way of boom economics.

Another car pushes into the gas station, the bell dings, and

Fritz-Peter doesn't want to lose this job too, so he runs out to pump gas, scrub windshields, soak up more oil under his fingernails, but before he runs, he sets Boris up with a little cup of coffee in the corner and tells him to wait, just wait.

"This Car Doesn't Brake for Liberals," announces the bumper. The car a definite antique.

CHAPTER 24

I like your hair. Why so glum? asks Lai Fun. She watches people filter in, mill around the door as though afraid to enter. Idiots. It's just a twenty-year reunion, not an execution. The bagpiper cancelled for a funeral.

No reason, says Stefanja.

Thor isn't coming?

Nope.

Lai Fun watches Stefanja hold a Jiffy Marker close to her nose for a long time.

Could I borrow that pen? asks Lai Fun, and Stefanja woozily hands the pen to her. Wow, says Lai Fun, popping the lid firmly back on the pen. Marianne's gained a lot.

Well, she's thirty-eight, says Stefanja distractedly. Not sixteen. Why should she look the same as she did when she was sixteen? I don't know why everyone's supposed to look the same as they did when they were sixteen. Except for your hair in a different style, you look like you did when you were sixteen, but that's just unnatural. That's just stupid. You done with that pen yet? No? Okay.

And Stefanja gets up from behind the table and stumbles

gracefully over to Marianne and they start gesticulating.

Stefanja oblivious and unaware that her husband is now meat, but keenly aware that she is a single parent, that she made a bad choice. The night before her twenty-year reunion. He was not a bad man, only a stupid man; the praise he received in his life more damaging than if a single person had told him he was a terrible writer, a singularly unimaginative filmmaker.

Lai Fun doesn't know anything, not about the note, not about the trip. And her mother called her just before she left. Lai Fun, you must come to dinner tomorrow, and Lai Fun couldn't believe that her mother had *forgotten* that tomorrow was Day Two of the reunion.

Lai Fun, this is a Dinner. You can't skip a Dinner.

You've never cared about my life, says Lai Fun. You've only ever cared about your life and Daddy's.

Lai Fun, it's your Heritage.

Really.

We need to borrow your house, says Louve. You have a big enough dining room table.

How many people?

I don't know. Ten? Eleven?

They gonna clean up after?

Lai Fun, you are speaking to your mother.

Well, mother, I don't feel like having a party, because I am in the middle of my twenty-year *reunion*.

And Fritz-Peter tells Louve not to push it, especially since they'll be eating Lai Fun's lover for dinner. Try convincing her later tonight, says Fritz-Peter. When she's come home from her reunion and she's all bummed out because it was awful.

Lai Fun doesn't know anything, but she will know Thor by the yellowy taste of nicotine under the shrimp-shell fingernails, the after-taste in the soup, and will be furious with her mother; secretly relieved that she didn't have to kill him herself because she was *this* close to putting him down.

Stefanja finishes talking to Marianne, then glides over to the name-tag table where she makes up a tag for Marianne who for some reason doesn't have a tag made up for her. Stefanja makes up tags for several people – Zevon, Haroun, Dennis, last minute arrivals who plunk down their money – and she smiles vaguely and points them in the direction of the bar and the buffet table. She finds Daisy's name-tag, shoos Daisy into the reception area by the bar.

Daisy. Stefanja pretends not to know Daisy, even when Daisy says, You're Lai Fun's neighbour now, right? I remember you.

Stefanja re-alphabetizes name-tags and straightens out the sign-in sheets to hide the fact that she is husbandless. She hands out more name-tags, tests the sound system, harasses the bartender for making her Caesar too spicy. Then she remembers something very important about Zevon. And Haroun. And Dennis. She almost rams the Jiffy Marker up her nose.

She's slept with all of them.

Lai Fun in her black leather maternity pants she had specially made – she still has a great, if expanded, ass – hands out cards that cleverly enough have Xeroxed yearbook photos on them next to the name. This idea was Jennifer Singh's, who had one of those rare flashes of genius that made Lai Fun fall in love with her in the first place.

Lloyd Weaselhead phoned her this morning to say the restaurant was short-staffed and he would be setting up the food for the catering van until at least five and for her to start without him and Maureen. She gave the telephone receiver the finger and said as sweetly as honey or maltose syrup in the morning, So when will you be there?

When we get there, he said. Duh, he added, then laughed.

Bonsoir, Lai Fun! Do you remember me? Do you still speak

French? shouts Mlle Tremblay at Lai Fun. Is there a name-tag for me somewhere?

Mlle Tremblay! Bonsoir! My French is terrible. I'm sorry. No reflection on you.

Je m'appelle Violet! Pas Mlle Tremblay, says Mlle Tremblay. Mlle Tremblay's hair wound up in a grey bun on top of her head, her body in a heavy purple gown.

Bonsoir Mlle Violet! shouts Lai Fun. Lai Fun didn't remember inviting teachers.

Comment ça va?

Ça va bien, she says. Ça va très bien, merci!

She wonders if her accent is as bad as she thinks. She wonders if she will have to have this conversation again and again tonight.

Alors, bonjour tout le monde, says a woman behind Mlle Tremblay in a flowery Laura Ashley dress, spritzed bangs, and huge plastic earrings.

Lai Fun never said it was an eighties retro reunion.

Umm, says Lai Fun, the perfect bilingual, bicultural Canadian. What's your name? I'm sorry. I just don't remember you.

Lisa Guiterrez, says the woman. The flowers leave her voice. We were best friends in Grade Two.

Oh, of course! I remember you now, good to see you! You haven't changed a bit, ha ha ha! Just let me find your name-tag.

Lai Fun tries not to let her cheeks puff out from the hot air of the lie. The first of many that night. She looks over to where Stefanja is supposed to be helping with name tags; Stefanja is doodling a chain saw on a napkin. Lai Fun decides to leave Stefanja alone.

Lai Fun moves through the crowd with her huge stomach and gigantic tits, the red carpet of her endometrium rolling out before her among the reunionites.

Shit! the bartender says. When are you due? Yesterday?

He looks at her thighs, reaches out, pats her hand.

Oops. I apologize if you're not pregnant.

I'm pregnant, Lai Fun snarls.

The bartender takes her tone as a hormonal thing. He will not let the pregnant woman's nasty energy make him crabby.

Hormones, the Baked Potatoes whisper as Lai Fun growls and sulks and frowns into her apple juice, into their softened, wrinkled, chewed-up faces. Stefanja stands beside them, watching Lai Fun, wondering what Lai Fun Kugelheim thinks she's wearing.

Lai Fun sees the following nametags:

Andrew (figure-skater who had a corn problem), Patty (a baby at seventeen), Gary (so much acne his face was one big zit, played the trombone, when she asked, refused to go to the graduation dance with her), William (mother from Fiji, had a perm all through senior high, dad lost his job and they had to move to Libya), Sharon (Catholic, mole on her left cheek), Omar (perm, mother looked like a European model, dad lost his job, wouldn't go to the graduation dance with her), Vanessa (six feet tall in Grade Nine and a Goth in Grade Twelve, dad lost his job and became a consultant), Dimitri (refused to go to the graduation dance with Lai Fun, said he'd never date someone from a different race in Social Studies class even though his brother dated a Chinese girl, had b.o.), Anne (even though she was petite, blonde, and had boobs, she was still a big weirdo who wore a giant cross on a necklace, she gave Lai Fun the shivers – petite blonde girls wearing crosses always make Lai Fun shiver).

She watches Alain, who owns a software company, exchange a business card with Aileen, a lawyer with the firm Forsch, Dudek, and Deckert. Pam, now an engineer, schmoozes with Seabird, now also an engineer. Hugo says he's between jobs and no one talks to him so he says it again into his gin and tonic.

Lai Fun watches the cloud of collective amnesia settle on the crowd. She was happy for a moment in her halter-top and fancy hair and then she saw them all and it crashed into her again that she didn't like high school all that much, in fact she hated high school and surely she can't be the only one who remembers the shit-ball time in high school? And who in the frig does Stefanja Dumanowski think she is, anyway – you can take the girl out of the Baked Potatoes, but you can't take the Baked Potatoes out of the girl.

This is what Lai Fun believes. This is why you should pay attention because Lai Fun knows the truth: All those happy-ending, high-school-reunion movies are capital-c Crap. The truth shall set you free. Reunions are fun if your spousoid is the one reunionizing and you're only along for the ride and even then you're stuck in conversations that go nowhere but in sour cream kruller spirals. Or they're fun if you were popular and happy in high school and now you're so successful you shit gold doubloons, but what kind of mutant is that? Truly happy in school and then truly happy as an adult? Barf.

People have barfed plenty the day before a reunion, men fretting about hair plugs and promotions, women about how much weight they've gained since graduation. So why go? Just in case they *miss something.* To see how awful everyone else looks. To say I have four sons, to show off their wedding rings, to remember how Duane projectile-vomited onto the windshield and the rear-view mirror in Bogg's car on grad night. Never to say how nothing has changed since high school, nothing at all.

I wouldn't be here if I was single, says Angelina Angelini to Stefanja. Because it would just be the same old same old.

Hmm, says Stefanja, whose husband eloped with his mother the day before. She looks around for her old friends, Heather and Maureen.

She sees Lai Fun scrambling with a fallen piece of streamer, her face sweaty and shiny above her gigantic stomach and Stefanja remembers that Lai Fun was always such a dork and not a thing has changed about her in twenty years.

Reunions are only truly good if you're too old or too dead to remember what happened and have started accidentally pouring coffee into your morning cereal. Or gone to take a piss and mistaken the waste-basket for the toilet. Which you also did back in Grade Eleven, but then it was just funny instead of frightening.

If you're old enough, you don't give jack-shit about fluttering around the assholes you went to school with forty years ago or sixty years ago and it's just nice to go to a party where you know some people, and you know what? You lost your job, your wife divorced you, and you're a greeter at Wal-Mart, and those are just the fucking facts of life. Maybe your eldest daughter won't let you see your grandchild any more, told you so yesterday on the phone and hung up, but what-the-fuck-ever. Pass the white wine spritzer. Pass the Jack Daniels on the rocks. Pass the Labatt's Lite. Pass the fizzy water because once an alcoholic, always an alcoholic.

Or then there's the urban reunion myth about the fat girl turned gorgeously skinny and wearing leopard-print pants and every married thirty-eight-year-old male in the room sliding his wedding band into his wallet as she walks by with her Bloody Mary, or the girl everyone called Flatso in Grade Nine who's turned so buxom her tits could knock your eyeballs out. Or the loser who wore a shirt with 69 on it who was a big, fat virgin when he graduated, who's now a successful Executive Something married to the gorgeous head of Channel 7 who of course didn't go to your school. Because girls have to be married and fertile and boys have to have fertile wives and their own businesses. Reunion rules.

But these myths, as Lai Fun would tell you, are exactly myths and nothing more.

Maybe.

Maybe you're at a reunion and you see a huddle of stiff, salon-fresh hairdo's who, one at a time, each look at you like they're not looking at you, and as you go by on your way to the cash bar for a thirteenth drink, you hear: There's Stefanja. No, I'm over it now. And you can't remember what you did but you know it's probably bad, maybe you deserve to have an acid stomach. Like Stejanja Dumanowski's is right now.

Lai Fun feels like the Grinch in Whoville – she wants to grab them all by the eyelids and yank their eyeballs *open* to see that school wasn't fun, school was a horror movie. Haven't they seen those car-crash, serial killer high school movies? What happened between the movies and adulthood? Even Daisy has forgotten how horrible it was to find her biology textbook pages meticulously glued together with gum, to be the very first girl to develop breasts and have them mauled in the hallways by eyes and hands – her chest the Rocky Mountains sprung up overnight in the middle of a long stretch of fried-egg nipple prairie. The only people worth talking to aren't at the reunion. The people who wouldn't talk to Lai Fun in high school still won't talk to her. Just: Are you married?

Where are all the gay people? She could stand with them. Surely not every single one of them is still heterosexual.

No one ever says, I'm a waiter. I've been a waiter this whole time.

All the waiters stay home.

Among the missing: a lot of the so-called headbangers like Keith Chan and Michael Silver. Erin Finnegan the other lesbian. Julia G., the pot-head. Only one of the two sets of twins, Bernice and Bob, have shown up, but Bernice and Bob were always goody-four-shoes and would be upset if they weren't on time for their own executions. The evil set of twins, Leslie and Morris, probably detained for questioning in Texas or something. Morris always looked cute in a pompadoured, Morrissey from the Smiths kind of way. Hadley Constable. Hadley Constable, face softer around the edges, and a definite wattle forming under her chin between two genuine diamond earrings, sent word through her lawyer that she wouldn't be able to make the reunion – she's in jail for cocaine trafficking, but it's all a misunderstanding just like it was ten years ago, she's always targeted, targeted only because she's rich and her father is a judge. And Kim Shisamoto? Well, she's just plain ol' *dead*.

In high school they weren't this happy, why are they suddenly all so darn happy? Who said they could be so stupidly happy? She elbows in and starts to complain to Andrew and Aileen about how awful school was, remember the zits and the perms and the shitty teachers and the bullies (like Connie and Heather and Maureen who pushed her into the boys' washroom once) and isn't it great it's over, but no one joins her complaint chorus. Instead Zoe Deckert, the girl whose boyfriend at the time laughed when she broke both her arms and legs after she rode her bike into the back of his car in Grade Eleven, smiles and sighs, Isn't it great? To see everyone again?

Lai Fun realizes that just as she was a mutant in school, so is she a mutant now.

Seeing all these people really makes you happy, Zoe?

Yes. Aren't you happy?

What about that guy over there? Isn't that the kid who wrote you a fake love letter that you believed and read it out loud to his friends in Biology class? Isn't that Simon McMillan, the guy who horked on your head in the stairwell? You happy to see him?

And then Zoe gets flustered and blushy so Lai Fun says, Maybe what you really mean is that you're happy he's lost all his hair. Maybe that's what you mean.

And Zoe says something about how she doesn't remember that, and We were teenagers, teenagers do silly things, that was so long ago. Have you seen my husband, my drink? I should go find him, it. So great seeing you again, Lai Fun. Really.

And Zoe scurries away from Lai Fun's face perched like a vulture over her silver halter-top pregnancy.

Lai Fun knows they think she is a truly negative person capable of carrying grudges for twenty years, a person who wants everyone to be miserable *just like her.*

Hello Stefanja, she says to Stefanja Dumanowski, no longer her best friend since university, but just one of the many bitches who went to her school. Stefanja plain as ever, only now with wrinkles around her shiny lipstick and her hair dyed toilet-disinfectant blue. So Thor left you for his mother. That's too bad. Really. I feel bad for you. Goodbye.

She's gotten her own back at stupid Stefanja Dumanowski. Lai Fun takes a deep breath. Demands a glass of tonic water this time. And where is Lloyd Weaselhead? He's late with the dinner and she's ready finally to tell him off for coming out of the closet in front of her all those years ago and then him ignoring her and acting like it hadn't happened for the next twenty years. She wants to throw her fizzy drink on his expensive leather shoes.

Lai Fun looks at all the pictures up around her of football victories, professional-looking snapshots from the Grade Twelve production of *The Mikado*. Someone, probably Maureen Weaselhead, has even put up Japanese-themed, painted parasols and fans on the walls. Lai Fun takes a long, pregnant gulp of her tonic. She needs a bathroom *now.*

Lloyd Weaselhead walks in the door, his arm around Maureen, and he's brought the food and a television crew with him. Lai Fun watches as they follow him around with their video cameras. Lloyd Weaselhead is having his reunion shot for a documentary about him, Lloyd Weaselhead.

She is about to shout until his eardrums implode when she spots Daisy talking to the DJ. Daisy. The first girl Lai Fun ever kissed.

Lai Fun realizes at the age of thirty-eight that she is ready to face her demons. She wants to show off her success before her life changes again. Forget that even though she makes excellent money – money is not the problem – she is fucking her neighbour's husband, not fucking her own wife at all while still being fucked over by her wife, Thor's wife probably fucking Angélique (not that Angélique would ever tell, Angélique never even mentioned Marguerite, Angélique never mentions any girlfriends ever). Her mother sharing afternoon drinks with that fuckwit Thor. She is dying to confront Lloyd Weaselhead here in the place where he made her the most miserable. She wants to talk to him, then maybe eviscerate him.

But she's in the community hall, not the school, and she takes a long sniff of Jiffy Marker to turbo-charge herself awake. A strange, ancient smell in the brand new community hall. The corners of the main room smell like sandstone. The metallic bathroom like Murphy's oil soap. Like floor wax, like little kid's vomit, like teenage angst. The smell of the huge, steep staircases of her old school.

She doesn't like these old building smells invading her head. Where's the toilet?

Lai Fun asks the bartender for mineral water in a hi-ball glass.

The sex Lai Fun has with Thor has a lot to do with her pregnancy-accelerated libido. But Lai Fun has decided that sex with Thor has even more to do with Stefanja being an old Baked Potato who ignored Lai Fun just like all the Potatoes ignored Lai Fun. Everything to do with a very dumb, hot-skinned Thor lying ready at attention when her hormones require a body, Jennifer's body off at work aiming to be the next Gargoyle VP, and Lai Fun needing until she will implode.

(LAI FUN washes her hands in the bathroom sink with pink soap and water so hot it steams out of the sink. A woman enters.)

ANGELINA ANGELINI

Lai Fun?

LAI FUN

Angelina?
(trying not to notice Angelina's outrageous nose-job)
You look great!

ANGELINA

So do you! When are you due?
(looks at LAI FUN's wedding rings)
Oh my god, when did you get married?

LAI FUN

Two years ago. We have a little boy, Frederick.

ANGELINA

Is your husband here? What does he do? Can I meet him?

LAI FUN

No, she's not here. She works for Gargoyle.

ANGELINA

Oh. And another one on the way! When are you due?

LAI FUN

Ten minutes ago.

(LAI FUN and ANGELINA give each other big car bumper smiles.
CONNIE CLARKE-LARKE walks in.)

CONNIE CLARKE-LARKE
Angelina?

ANGELINA
Connie? Oh my god, Connie, you look great!

CONNIE
So do you! Your nose looks so good!

(Both the POTATOES continue to talk to each other. LAI FUN picks up
her drink from the counter and flushes it down the toilet.)

Anne Winters, gaunt like someone who's aerobicized too much,
her body wiry and bug-eyed, the silver cross still clasped tightly
around her throat. A balding Dennis Chong and his paunch almost as big as Lai Fun's stomach ogling her tits through the
spangly top. Lai Fun wants to ask him when he's due and, oh
yeah, didn't he refuse to go to the graduation dance with her?
Brigitte Anderson looking hot in leopard-print pants and long
purple nails. Billy Briscoe, perfectly egg bald. Lai Fun looks
around at all her old school-mates and sees nothing she didn't
already expect, except that so many of them are dead.

Marianne, for example, killed herself after she got an A-
on her English departmental exam. Haroun threw himself out
an office building window on Black Monday. Zevon was elec-
trocuted on a film set. Anne – well, no one's quite sure how
Anne Winters died. A grisly, unsolved murder somewhere in
California.

Bloody crashers.

On the other hand, why shouldn't they come? Except that

they weren't invited officially – Lai Fun feels ambiguous about it, and a little irritated when she sees them at the buffet table helping themselves when there's only a certain amount of food for the eighty or so scheduled to come. It's not like the dead need to eat – they're just eating because everyone else is.

But she doesn't want to go hurting dead people's feelings. It must be hard enough. She invited some of the dropouts, but she didn't invite the dead ones. On the other hand, they somehow found out about it, so what can she do? And what about all the crashers who think this is some kind of dress-up party and have arrived in costumes? She's already counted two nuns and three old-fashioned nurses with little caps on their heads and navy blue capes flung over their shoulders. And what about that idiot dressed up like a motorcycle crash victim carrying his head in a helmet under his arm? Not very funny at all. Should she stand at the door and tell them not to come in? No, too late. But they got in free! They better not try to hog the buffet table. The music's started already, so maybe people will ease off the food and just dance. She feels a little like a bride who's noticed the people from the wildlife conference downstairs dancing at her reception. Flattered. Annoyed.

She sees the fourth captain of the football team still in his uniform. Heart attack at age eighteen. One of the Gifted Class. Snorted coke.

Ozzie the Mennonite, whom they say masturbated himself to death.

Of course the dead have come – only the dead would have boring enough lives to *look forward* to a high school reunion.

They heard her call and they clustered on the other side of death's doorway ready for the appointed day. Lai Fun's fingers pressed and depressed the buttons on her phone a little too hard, she commanded her computer search a little too thoroughly. While she planned out her slinky, black evening frock with a black shawl thrown over the shoulder and lots of gold jewellery then changed her mind to the halter top and black leather pants, the dead assembled themselves, sent her their RSVPS via dust messages on her car, put condoms in the basement bathroom, hid the toilet paper, ripped open the bottoms of her grocery bags, dumped her keys into the gutter.

She's read about this before – the ways the dead contact the living. They hide the end portion on the roll of Scotch tape. Stash away eyeglasses and keys, make the fuse blow when the kettle and the hair-dryer are plugged in at the same time. All this has been happening to her, all the time, as well as an over-riding need to constantly pee.

Haroun starts to cut a jig in the middle of the dance floor. He is drunk, he's been dancing with all the women except his widow. Even though he's drunk, his dancing is good – easy, perfectly rhythmical – and he moves his hips side-to-side and around and forward and backward like a belly-dancing fertility god. Haroun, the stock specialist who couldn't cope – his mother was a dancer with the Royal Winnipeg Ballet, dancing is in his genes, in his jeans, and he dances by himself for an entire song because he is drunk enough and happy enough to be here among the living.

Lai Fun gets up and in her black leather pants also starts to dance, but not with Haroun because she saw him double-dip a whole handful of carrots. She too dances by herself, no, she dances with her baby, holds her stomach in her arms, starts to sway. Ozzie pogos in from the bathroom, he pogos past the bar, past the memorial table, onto the dance floor and jumps straight up and down and up and down; Daisy glides on to the dance floor, all long-limbed and lyrical; Paul limbos into the spotlight, knees first. Lai Fun, the ultimate lezbo of the Grade Twelve Graduating Class; Haroun, the management failure; Ozzie the masturbator; Daisy the anorexic poet; Paul the boy who got the biggest wedgie in the world and still lived. The dumbo kids from the Orange Group. Dancing in the centre of attention.

The Baked Potato People and the Trojans stop the music, and Corby gets on stage. Stone griffins flank both ends of the stage. Corby tests the mic, even though Stefanja already tested it a dozen times before and yelled at the DJ three times: One two, one two, can everyone hear me?

But the crowd's clatter is too loud. Zevon balances a drink on his forehead and starts spinning around. Zevon, the human top.

Hello? Hello? calls Corby Knudsen. Hey! Listen up! I want to talk about that season final game we played against St Ignatius –

Maureen Weaselhead takes the mic from Corby. People will listen to her, she was one of the Gifted Class, she is Lloyd Weaselhead's wife, after all.

I want to take everyone down a special path off Memory Lane, it's called *The Mikado*, she says. Remember *The Mikado*? The Japanese theme for this dance is in commemoration of that show that took place in our graduating year. The biggest audiences the school had ever seen – and three of us are going to perform the final number which we've been rehearsing for – everyone? Everyone? Could you please settle down?

But the crowd gets louder. Haroun not only continues his jig but starts to sing in his beautiful *Man of La Mancha* voice; Anne Winters shows off some tae kwon do moves for Marianne and accidentally knocks Zevon's rum and Coke off his forehead and kicks a hole in the wall. A Japanese parasol crashes to the floor. Anne and Marianne and Zevon laughing like goofs because they're tipsy and the drinks are half-price. Stefanja murmurs to Zevon about the dress Hadley Constable wore to graduation and how it made Hadley look like a black-forest cake. Zevon laughs so hard he bends over and clutches his knees. Stefanja laughs into her hands.

The Trojans and the Potatoes flutter and stomp around on the stage. They make a Popular People's huddle; occasionally a face appears, a chin, an elbow, a jowl, a shiny forehead, a twin set of crow's feet. They are in pieces – an arm here, a leg jiggling, and many mouths, some stained by years of drinking and cigarettes and raising children, most of them clumped with pink lipstick in the corners, or lipstick on the teeth, eyebrows plucked like wealthy chickens. The Trojans' voices are too loud, but not loud enough, their fingers too stubby with scrubby islands of hair on the digits and too-big pores on the hands and faces. Wide-spaced teeth. Lai Fun notices a griffin parked Stage Left.

Kim Shisamoto walks in. Stefanja Jiffy-Marks her a name-tag and asks what she's been up to. Kim Shisamoto, who died of cancer just eight months ago and started the whole reunion train because she didn't want a funeral, she wanted to be buried in peace.

I'm dead, Potato-Head, Jesus Christ, who cares what I've been up to, says Kim. Hank, is that you? You freckled ass, give me a hug! Where's the fucking music? What is this, fucking high tea with the Queen, we can't have some fucking music? What're those dorks doing on the stage? Oh gawd, not more of that Mikado shit!

Kim pushes over a fake rice-paper screen.

Hank, you fucker! she shouts. You knocked me up! I told you those condoms were past their expiry date! Ha ha ha!

Hank, his stomach round, his head bald, sweeps Kim into his arms and swings her around and around.

Haroun gyrates his hips and opens his arms to Paul, Ozzie, Daisy, Lai Fun, and Kim. Except for Lloyd Weaselhead, the Orange Group together again.

Haroun's hair cut short because he was in the money business after all, but a single, heavy curl bobbing on his forehead as he dances in the centre of a circle of people along with Lai Fun. The damp scent of his rich cologne. Marianne jumps into the middle of the circle and does the high school two-step, from side to side just off the beat, her shoulders hunched to hide her new tits. When "I Will Survive" comes on, she lets out a whoop and throws her arms up into the air. Anne Winters does some kicky-punchy dance moves in her Italian leather high-heeled boots and dances across from Marianne because even though both of them are dead, they both Will Survive.

The waves of old music edge up around Lai Fun's body and she swims, floating the musical notes, the decades-old bass guitar and synthesized violin riffs. But then the waves rise to her chest and the music squeezes her lungs, laps at her chin, her mouth, her nose. She treads frantically, tries to shout, scream, but the music presses at her lungs. She loses air, her balance, her throat muscles because she sees Mrs Blake. She stops dancing.

Lai Fun put Mrs Blake out of her mind, away from the front of her brain long ago.

Lai Fun, says Kim. Snap. Out. Of it. That was over twenty years ago.

Mrs Blake! shouts Kim. Come on and dance!

There's Lloyd Weaselhead! Kim shouts. With a camera crew. Hilarious. What a buffoon. This is great! What a great idea! A reunion!

Lloyd Weaselhead dances towards them, Mrs Blake dancing up behind him.

CHAPTER 25

Mrs Blake lazily opens her eyes under the pounds and pounds of clay and peat and earth and hybrid tea rose roots. Her eyes spread open and she touches her throat – the singing, the echo of howling above her: You are invited, you are invited, sway the wires, the air, she has been invited and the inviting pulls her up through the ground, her many pieces rising up through the earth and past the bushes and up into the air, she has been invited becn invited been invited. . . .

CHAPTER 26

Lloyd's cameraman puts his camera down and heads to the bar. Lai Fun watches to make sure he doesn't try to help himself to any snacks. Lai Fun stomps around Lloyd and grabs Mrs Blake. She heads in the direction of the washrooms – washrooms are always good places to confront the enemy and bawl the truth out – but the washroom has a line-up, so she hustles Mrs Blake outside to the parking lot, around the building to the back over-looking the outdoor community swimming pool, to the park behind the condos. The moon is pathetic, not dark, not full, but some wishy-washy phase in between.

The smell of chalk dust, the bag of pencils that are Mrs Blake in Lai Fun's arms, makes her heart beat so hard it begins to dig its way out of her chest. Makes the fetus in her belly scrabble with fetus horns and talons. Fetus scrabbles on all sides of Lai Fun's uterus.

Mrs Blake sags onto the hood of a car, waits for Lai Fun to sit beside her.

Mrs Blake, Lai Fun decides, will never teach Lai Fun's baby. Or anyone's baby. Ever, ever again.

CHAPTER 27

Mrs Blake's Classroom: 1985

If you'd called ahead we could have booked an appointment, says Mrs Blake.

She carries a Mikado fan. Snaps it open and closed and covers her mouth, sometimes her eyes with the bright flowers and petrified birds.

You've been feeding on children, says Louve.

Louve's eyes feel too hot from the tears right behind them. Babies!

Mrs Blake seats herself behind her desk covered with paper and chalk and hair.

I am just doing my job, says Mrs Blake. Assimilating them. You parading around here like this is your home, like you were born here, like you own the rules. Who gets to feed on whom! Taking jobs away from people who deserve them and were here first. You are an invader. You're not only a creep and a bum, you're a monster and a freak.

I'm going to phone the School Board and the Police. I'm going to get you fired.

The School Board can't do anything, says Mrs Blake. I'm permanent. I'd have to kill a pupil before I lost my job. And I haven't done that. I never do that. I've been teaching here forever. I'm going to keep on teaching forever.

Louve lashes out her claws and swipes a gash on Mrs Blake's throat. Mrs Blake bites her fangs down into Louve's arm. Louve reaches around, snaps Mrs Blake's neck and Mrs Blake slides off the desk and lands on her chest among the papers, the broken sticks of chalk, the Mikado fans, the wigs piled with human hair.

Louve will bury Mrs Blake in her garden. Sow her into place with roses and herbs. Forget about her.

And now Lai Fun, and all the howling over a *reunion* of all things, has resurrected Mrs Blake.

Lai Fun starts to cry, her heart breaking because this night is turning out to be just a little too much. Some memories are not meant to be resurrected, some memories are better left buried in metaphors and bogs. A reunion co-opted by the Trojans and the Potatoes; her cheating on her beloved Jennifer whom she swore to love forever; a reunion where there isn't enough food for all the people because almost half of them are dead; her nice, normal, adult, neighbourly friendship with Stefanja fucked to hell; and now Mrs Blake who went missing all those years ago, suddenly showing up like this is all in honour of *her*. The Queen Wasp of Lai Fun's school-time misery. The founder of the *Mikado* fiasco. Lai Fun suddenly two feet tall and three-pig tails on her head again.

Mrs Blake, shouts Lai Fun. You simply cannot come to the reunion. You weren't invited!

Lai Fun tries to push up the slumping Mrs Blake.

Sit up, says Lai Fun. You can sit up by yourself. Don't play the invalid.

A reunion, says Mrs Blake. You invited me. That was so nice.

Lai Fun wants to gag from the smell of the chalk and brushes and mimeographs. Mrs Blake looks up at Lai Fun, her eyelids drooping coyly. She reaches towards Lai Fun's stomach.

Can I touch? she says, and she covers Lai Fun's belly with her hands. Fetus shifts and growls. Mrs Blake looks into Lai Fun's face.

You're all grown up now.

Lai Fun looks at Mrs Blake, shorter, smaller, thinner than Lai Fun ever remembered her. Lai Fun wipes the tears pouring from every orifice in her face.

Yes, says Lai Fun.

Lai Fun falls to her knees in the grass, her eyes pouring tears, her head pounding from the waves washing over her. She holds her stomach, topples over on to her side.

The Orange Group is all grown up now, whispers Lai Fun, her heart cracking. We all turned out all right.

Yes, you did, says Mrs Blake. You did just fine.

The music pumps inside the building, sweeps around the parking lot. "I Will Survive" for the fifteenth time because the Orange Group has kicked out the Potatoes and the Trojans. Lai Fun looks up into Mrs Blake's grey, wrinkled face. Mrs Blake reaches out her arms.

CHAPTER 28

Louve and Boris stir pots of Thor stock. Fritz-Peter rolls up pieces of blood sausage in slices of bacon.

Thyme! Louve barks. Fresh thyme!

We're out of thyme, says Fritz-Peter.

No, says Louve. I brought over a whole bagful from the garden.

He said it's all gone, says Boris.

Louve rhythmically stirs the pot. Boris, she says, did I ask your cake-hole?

Boris stares down into his pot. Wipes his sweaty forehead.

I'm going to run out back and get some from the garden, says Louve. You cake-holes stay here.

She wipes her hands on her apron and takes along a bread bag and scissors.

The closer she gets to the garden, the grumpier she feels and the sicker her stomach feels and she knows it's because she's been snacking too much with all the cooking, and drinking too much of the sparkling wine Thor brought over.

Sicker and sicker she feels, fully nauseated, she's almost ready to turn back even though the garden plot is just across the street, the thyme standing and waiting for the first snow, when she sees her garden destroyed, the mounds of earth scattered, her rose bush she planted the year Trudeau died and the herbs and the flowers uprooted and strewn on the gravel, she throws up, her body doubled over, her hands holding her cheeks, her face hot and damp and spewing out the raw meat, because she knows that in the bleeding green of the ruined rose bush Hilda Blake has escaped. Louve takes a breath, wipes her mouth on her apron and stumbles to the garden plot. She pokes the earth with her scissors.

Louve's head snaps up when she remembers Lai Fun's insane reunion call, the one that almost blasted out Louve's eardrums. Lai Fun's reunion. The children. Lai Fun could never deal with Mrs Blake on her own. Lai Fun doesn't have the heart for it. There's no time. Louve grabs a breast in each hand and breaks into a run.

Louve stops short at the site of the community hall. Around her she smells blood and bodies, she smells antiseptic and disease, collapsed dust of bricks and mortar, worse than ever before.

A Grey Nun swishes by, her habit leaving a wave of lye and blood. Louve helps a woman wheel her IV stand over the edge of the sidewalk, the IV needle driven into the woman's hand.

Do you work here? asks the woman. Could you get me some water for these flowers my son left?

After I save my daughter.

Louve! she hears from across the parking lot.

Joe! says Louve. Joe the last patient, the last body, the last day, Louve's hospital a cloud of dust and misery. You here too? Have you seen my daughter?

Of course I'm here. I couldn't not come. I was invited.

Got your tag on still I see. Have you seen my daughter?

You fastened the tag securely. Very good, says Joe. Last time

I heard, your daughter was in the embrace of a schoolteacher by the outdoor swimming pool.

Thank you, Joe!

Are you coming in? The music's very good. I'm feeling up to a little dancing.

Later! Louve calls.

Louve dives into the smell of the old hospital and runs around the building.

In the hall, Anne Winters has lifted the Trojan DJ up into the air and thrown him against the wall in the steamy, hot, dancing room. Nuns hug doctors, priests hug priests, patients do the IV jive. Football players hug computer nerds, drama guys hug Trojans and do pop-a-wheelies in wheelchairs, phlebotomists dip orderlies, interns twirl with housekeepers and janitors on their shoulders.

Louve studies the room from the doorway.

Mrs Blake dances with Lai Fun. It has been years since Mrs Blake danced, maybe she's never danced at all, she was too busy working, she never took enough time out, she should have danced more, should have swung her hair around her shoulders more. She hugs Lai Fun and Lai Fun gives her back an A hug, she strokes Lai Fun's stomach, shouts at Lai Fun that her baby will be a little girl, Lai Fun happy that she's finally realized she's thirty-eight and no longer eight, Mrs Blake just a woman, a woman with claws and fangs, but still essentially just a woman, and Louve screams when she sees them, Louve in the dancehall's doorway, balloons bobbing around her, Louve's hair wild, her apron flapping, she howls because that monster is touching her baby, poisoning her grandchild.

Lai Fun, get away from there! Get away from her! screams Louve, running towards them, running in horror movie slow motion.

224

Lai Fun hears her mother's voice.

Louve runs toward them, Lloyd Weaselhead runs behind Louve, a shish-kebab skewer in his hand, the TV crew behind.

Mrs Blake darts from Lai Fun's arms and out the door, her haunches strong and muscular, her wings wide and sandstone-old. She disappears into the trees, scrambles through the branches with her claws. She will dance more – from now on. This is her resolution. In her gargoyle beauty, she climbs into the sky.

Louve runs to Lai Fun and holds on to her knees while she tries to recover her breath.

Louve's breath slows, and she unwraps her arms from around Lai Fun. She stands up slowly. Wipes her forehead, looks at Lai Fun.

This is what you decided to wear? she asks.

Lloyd, you big homo, says Lai Fun. She has finally cornered Lloyd Weaselhead. Outside the bathroom. In front of a TV camera.

What are you doing still married to Maureen Jones? she asks. I saw you necking with Corby Knudsen in the drama room in Grade Twelve. I saw you!

Corby Knudsen? We played football! So what if I had him? And Andrew? And Dimitri?

So why are you married to Maureen? Why aren't you with a man? Why are you back in the closet?

What the hell are you talking about? Maureen doesn't give a shit about who I slept with before I married her. I loved her and I still love her – that's why I married her. I would never trade her in for a lunk-head like Corby Knudsen. What are you doing here, single? Everyone knows you married some woman. I can sleep with who I like. I'm not afraid of what *you* think.

Lai Fun crosses her arms. Hmph. Uncrosses her arms and puts her hands on her hips. Hmph.

She'll get Lloyd Weaselhead back at the forty-year reunion.

CHAPTER 29

The dinner is thirteen people big. Not very many left in the oil business; only two still married to the same people. The griffins from the bridge sit in the back garden, propped on either side of Freddy's swing-set. (Stay! said Lai Fun, patting their heads. Good griffins. Stay there! Good boys.) Gleaming bottles of red and white wine and sparkling water Lai Fun and Jennifer's donation to the dinner.

Slice with serrated steak knives through rare meat marinated in olives, capers, red wine, roasted in the oven until fragrant and perfect. Crunch through crackling, hint of rosemary, garlic, chew eagerly around the bone, suck out the fatty marrow. Smell the salt of the meat, the salt of the garlicky sauces in the little bowls over the tea lights, the slurp of skewers dipped into Thai peanut sauce, black bean sauce, black-pepper gravy, the sound of meat being chewed, the squeak and slice of incisors into the meat. Louve dips her fingers into a bowl of water and lemon slices, then wipes her hands on a napkin. Monsters are delicate eaters. Everyone knows this.

Fritz-Peter in his cowboy boots and cowboy hat. Louve in

a short, cute leather skirt of Lai Fun's, her thighs so exercised they flex by themselves.

How the grease of sauce and meat gets on their fingers and around their mouths and lipstick smears and drips onto napkins, on laps, and on the floor.

Lai Fun gives Stefanja a good look as Stefanja devours a brain fritter with her long fingers and her wet lips and sharp little teeth. Stefanja, Lai Fun's best friend again now that the reunion is pretty much over. Stefanja and Lai Fun will need to make up to each other for their crummy reunion behaviour; a day at the spa downtown with iced coffee at the end or something. Just the two of them. Without the kids. Like back in university. Commerce 201.

Lai Fun sits beside Jennifer Singh and Jennifer hardly recognizes her in the candlelight. Her beautiful Lai Fun who made a token nibble at a black-bean finger, then sneaked it on to Jennifer's plate; Lai Fun who prefers her slice of baked tofu because to her tofu is a little bit of heaven. Jennifer took an evening off work, just this once, because she knew it was important to Lai Fun, because she knew Fritz-Peter had some interesting oil connections from back when he was in the oil business, and she's seated herself neatly between Freddy and some high-powered lawyer she's never heard of. Jennifer's riding high on the crest of this economic boom – it all makes sense in terms of economics. So she's taken the night off to spend with her family to give her life some balance.

Lai Fun tries not to look at the table strewn with the roasted and fried and fricasseed parts of her ex-lover. Instead she looks at Jennifer, feeding bits of boiled carrot to their son. She married Jennifer and when she did she made several vows, none of which she has bothered to follow lately. Her Jennifer. Hers. She has to start remembering that.

Lai Fun will name the baby Daisy.

No, says the fetus. Marguerite.

She dips the last chunk of tofu into the dish of soy sauce and puts it in her mouth. She takes a sip of Italian mineral water.

She is dying for a scotch.

This is the way of the city.

CHAPTER 30

Louve pulls out her pad, her father's antique pen. First she writes the address on the envelope, then she licks the stamp and applies it to the upper right hand corner of the envelope. She would never waste a perfectly good envelope and stamp, so she will send the letter for sure this time. She tries again:

Dear Ann Landers,

I recently had old friends whom I hadn't seen in years over for a reunion dinner. I noticed at the party that although it was good to see all my old friends, I have definitely moved on while most of them seem stuck in the past and now they keep calling me wanting to get together for coffee, jogs in the park, séances, and on my nerves to rehash old times. Really Ann, I am at my wit's end trying to find a nice way to tell them to leave me alone. What advice can you give me regarding how to tell them to bug off, but in a way that won't hurt their sensitive feelings? I wouldn't mind seeing them at the next reunion, just not now.

Signed, A Reluctant Reunionite

Suzette Mayr is the author of the novels Moon Honey *(finalist for the Georges Bugnet Award for Best Novel and finalist for the Henry Kreisel Award for Best First Book) and* The Widows *(finalist for the Commonwealth Prize for Best Book, Canadian–Caribbean region). Her poetry and short fiction have appeared in numerous periodicals and anthologies and she has collaborated on projects with visual artists. She lives and works in Calgary.*

photo: Solo